THE RISING SON

The life of the Twenty was rigid, every minute controlled and scrutinized, but Dulok secretly met with his mother every week to plan their escape from the City of Kings.

One night, in the middle of their rendezvous, the door burst open; there stood Ornon and Dulok's half brother, Buz, who cried, "He has broken the Shadzean law! He is weak, unfit to be the Survivor, and he must be destroyed!"

"Silence!" Ornon snapped. "*I* will decide what must be done here. You can be assured that Dulok will suffer greatly for this."

And with his words, two soldiers entered the small room, each grabbing one of Dulok's arms. The young prince struggled vainly, only to witness the cold monarch drive the sharpened tip of his sword into his mother's heart.

On that terrible night, his destiny became clear: he would survive at all cost, so that he might stand on the day of the Reckoning. And after that, he would destroy Buz and Ornon mercilessly, for only then would the life of his gentle mother be avenged . . .

Don't Miss These Heroic Fantasy Favorites

RO-LAN #1: MASTER OF BORANGA   (616, $1.95)
by Mike Sirota

Swept into a strange, other dimensional world, Ro-lan is forced to fight for his life and the woman he loves against man, beast, and the all-powerful evil dictator, the **MASTER OF BORANGA**.

RO-LAN #2: THE SHROUDED WALLS OF BORANGA
by Mike Sirota   (677, $1.95)

Love and loyalty drive fearless and dashing Ro-lan to return to the horrifying isle of Boranga. But even if he succeeds in finding and crossing through the warp again, could he hope to escape that evil place of strange and hostile creatures?

THE TWENTIETH SON OF ORNON   (685, $1.95)
by Mike Sirota   —

Dulok, the twentieth son of Ornon, is determined to become the Survivor—the sole ruler of the mighty kingdom of Shadzea. But he is also determined to avenge the death of his mother—whose blood was spilled by the great Ornon himself!

THREE-RING PSYCHUS   (674, $1.95)
by John Shirley

The year is 2013 A.D. and the human race is faced with total destruction—or moving into the next stage of psychic development, the Great Unweighting: a partial cancellation of gravity, the destruction of cities, and the death of countless people.

THE TWENTIETH SON OF ORNON

BY MIKE SIROTA

ZEBRA BOOKS
KENSINGTON PUBLISHING CORP.

ZEBRA BOOKS

are published by

KENSINGTON PUBLISHING CORP.
21 East 40th Street
New York, N.Y. 10016

THE TWENTIETH
SON OF ORNON

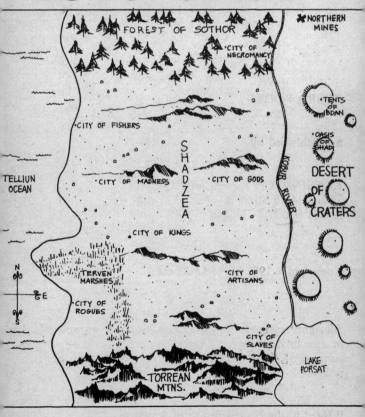

AUTHOR'S NOTE

THE TWENTIETH SON OF ORNON is not the first book I ever penned, nor is it the first to find print. But it is *my* personal favorite among the many stories that I've so far consigned to paper during my career, and accordingly I wish to dedicate it to *my* personal favorite among authors, the true Master of adventure fantasy, Edgar Rice Burroughs. It was ERB's incomparable works that unfettered my own imagination, as well as those of so many others. I offer this in gratitude for the worlds that he created, and in deep respect for his memory.

CHAPTER ONE

THE RITE OF THE TWENTY

It was the day of the Relinquishment.

The most knowledgeable merchant in the marketplace of the City of Kings knew this, as did the untutored peasant in one of Shadzea's distant rural provinces. None had been called to witness the proceedings, for this singular time belonged to a select few. But none felt slighted; on the contrary, they were gratified to know that the Rite of the Twenty, the oldest and most significant tradition in the long history of Shadzea, had progressed this far, for this was as it should be.

One by one the princes of Shadzea, Ornon's many sons, were led into the courtyard of the palace by their respective mothers, whom they would see that day for the last time. Ornon himself was there to observe the Relinquishment, though the morose king, his mind focused on more pressing matters of his reign, barely acknowledged the passage of the silent youths. That he had followed the same path years before meant little to the fourteenth Survivor of Shadzea, whose chest would not swell with pride until all but one of those whom he had sired lay dead.

What did these unsmiling youths, all just past the end of their eighth year of life, know or care of the traditions that had brought them to this place and time? It had not been the task of their mothers to instruct them in the history of Shadzea, but rather to guide them swiftly through the earliest years of their existence, and also to implant in their impressionable minds the most rudimentary seeds of awareness regarding what the gods had predestined for them. They would learn all else of necessity from their individual mentors, under whose wing they would fall from the day of the Relinquishment until the black night of their deaths. Yes, they would learn.

They would learn of Offow, sovereign of a smaller, less powerful Shadzea that struggled for its existence over four centuries ago. Under Offow's strong rule the kingdom was able to hold its own against its fierce neighbors, even expand its blood-soaked boundaries upon occasion. But Offow himself knew that the demise of Shadzea was as near as the last beat of his heart, for the heirs given him by his weak-willed queen were two simpering, effeminate sons. Left in their limp hands, Shadzea would become a forgotten paragraph in the history of some other land, unless Offow rectified the situation, something which he swore he would do.

While still a vital man of thirty-five, Offow initiated the Rite of the Twenty. This ceremony, so well honed to perfection that even through the reign of Ornon it remained virtually unchanged, commenced with the Mating Week, when fifty of Shadzea's most suitable young women were selected for him by his advisors. After a self-imposed abstinence of a month he dispatched

10

his not unpleasant obligations, the fruits of his efforts soon evident as all but two bore his seed.

Months later, during the Birth of Princes, Offow and his advisors were on hand to examine each infant. All males that showed deformity or sickness were sent to the red priests of Doj and Bao for sacrifice, as were the female infants. Only the healthy males were considered suitable. After his twentieth son was born, Offow declared the Birth of Princes at an end. All subsequent children, regardless of gender or health, were carried off by the red priests.

The Twenty now embarked on their singular path in life, the path that would lead to death for all, save one— the Survivor. For the first eight years each child remained with its respective mother, whose duties, according to the dictates of Offow, were to help the child grow, to begin instilling in him the earliest instincts of survival. There was no love, no emotion shared, and none objected when the child was taken away. They simply returned to their original duties after the day of the Relinquishment.

Individual mentors now guided the destinies of the princes for the duration of their lives, however long or short they were. The princes ate together, played together, and slept beneath the same roof. Friendships were discouraged, though the hatred and suspicion of others imparted to them so early by their mothers was more than enough to prevent this. The mentors taught them to use their minds, while soldiers trained them in physical prowess and arms. Many a would-be Survivor fell early in rough play, never to rise again. To the others this was as it should be, and none would proffer as much as a second glance to their fellow as he was carried from

11

the courtyard.

The first of the Princes' Trials came near the end of the maturing youths' fourteenth year. Both they and their mentors were escorted by Shadzean soldiers to Lake Porsat, then within the borders of their enemy. Upon a galley designated for the occasion they were rowed to the center of the deep lake, where each was assigned the task of diving below and retrieving one of the brilliant blue porsat blossoms, the flower that gave the lake its name. It seemed simple enough, and yet two never again saw the surface. None could say for sure that these drownings were anything more than the accidents they appeared to be.

The second and third Princes' Trials occurred at the end of the seventeenth and nineteenth years, each more difficult and dangerous than the preceding one, and by the end of the third trial the ranks of Offow's sons had dwindled to six. Now the princes were afforded more time with the king, and they were instructed in matters necessary to the survival of Shadzea. There was no love shared between father and son, for each knew his responsibility; each understood his respective purpose in life.

The fourth Princes' Trial occurred at the end of the twenty-second year, and was by far the most telling. Unlike the first three, where all performed the same task, the fourth trial, also called the Trial of Death, was an individual one. Each prince left the city on his own after announcing to Offow and his council the nature of his trial, and after receiving the king's sanction. No two were alike, although all were fraught with their own perils. When this trial was done, only three of the original Twenty had endured.

Those who survived the fourth Princes' Trial had but one obstacle left to overcome, the final step on their way to being proclaimed the Survivor. This was the day of the Reckoning, and it occurred near the end of the remaining princes' twenty-fourth year. In the vast courtyard, where as children they had played together years before, the princes met in direct confrontation. When the last drop of blood had been spilled, there was one remaining. Drenched in the lifeblood of himself and his brothers, reeking of sweat, Boga stood in the center of the courtyard and proclaimed himself the Survivor, the one most capable of ruling Shadzea. The name was spread throughout the troubled land, so that all might know of their future king. Offow then approached the first Survivor, and he embraced him symbolically. The Rite of the Twenty, begun with the Mating Week, was now ended.

They would learn, the young sons of Ornon, about Boga, the first Survivor, who became king of Shadzea not long after the day of the Reckoning, when Offow died. It was immediately evident that the long ritual conceived of by Offow had not been in vain, for he had left the kingdom in more than capable hands. Boga was ruthless, possessed of great intelligence, and even greater strength. With the enemies of Shadzea, whom he began to methodically crush, he was merciless. Many met unspeakable deaths, though the tortures that they endured at his hands made that death a welcome release.

Slowly, ever slowly, Boga extended Shadzea's borders outward from its capital, the city that later would be rebuilt in splendor and dubbed the City of Kings. Then, to the disbelief of many, the first Survivor formed a strange, terrifying alliance between himself and Sothor, the black magician, this all but assuring Shadzea's dominance for centuries to come. The shadowy Sothor, who claimed as his place of origin an unheard of land far to the south, was much feared, for all believed, contrary to what he claimed, that he had risen from the deepest pits of unholy Esh. His subsequent actions did little to dissuade them.

Under the aegis of the unlikely pair, the Shadzean army spread across the land like a rapidly darkening shadow. Sothor's enigmatic powers first terrified the enemy, addled his brain, weakened his will. Then, no longer able to resist, he fell easily to the crushing death blows of Boga and his fierce minions. Cities were pillaged, torn to the ground and rebuilt in the name of the Shadzean empire. Powerful kingdoms were pummeled into submission, until nothing was left, not even their once feared names.

For decades Shadzea had fought for its existence; now, in little more than a year, there were none left to challenge it. The kingdom that Boga had carved for himself extended for countless leagues in all directions from the site of the proposed capital. To the west it spread to the shores of the Telliun Ocean; to the south, as far as the unscalable Torrean Mountains; northward, to the edge of the vast northern forest; to the east, as far as the Kobur River. His new subjects, weak-kneed submissives all, were now honored to call themselves Shadzeans.

Before death cut short his reign, Boga was able to see the completion of the City of Kings, as well as to receive the second Survivor, his assurance that Shadzea's might would go unchallenged for another generation. But in his waning years the king was once again confronted by

Sothor, who had practiced his dark arts in the catacombs of the city since sequestering himself there after the conquest. Boga, though uneasy in his presence, knew all too well that the sorcerer's appearance portended the long awaited collection of his dues, for had he not promised him anything short of his soul for his help? Yet what could one such as he, ageless, without fear of death, desire of mortal man?

Before six days had passed, Boga had commissioned his artisans to begin work on a new city, for such was Sothor's request. It was to be a City of Necromancy, devoted solely to the teaching of the black arts to eager and willing acolytes, or so the sorcerer said. The very prospect of the cryptic place, less than two hundred miles northeast of the City of Kings, had made the unmoving Boga shudder, but he had calmly nodded his assent. If only he had not lived to know of its completion. . . .

They would learn, those who filed into the courtyard nervously before the cold stare of Ornon, about Dain, the second Survivor, and of the valorous deed that still shines above the many performed over the centuries by the long line of Shadzean monarchs. Dain, on his bloody path to the throne, had curried favor with the oft maligned red priests, who, in exchange for the promise of greater power, made numerous sacrifices to Doj and Bao on behalf of their champion. He had even proposed the building of huge temples, perhaps even a city, to honor the ancient Shadzean deities, and to learn of the construction of Sothor's foul city before his own nearly drove him to action. But he acceded to the advice of his mentors, and he bided his time.

Boga finally succumbed. Dain, within minutes of

scattering his father's ashes to the wind, summoned the red priests, and by nightfall the contingent, armed with amulets and urns, were many miles from the capital. They rode steadily, and before dawn of the fifth day they had reached the low hills surrounding the City of Necromancy. Dain knew that the dark arts were practiced in the night, when the demons of Esh were the most receptive. The early morning hours would find Sothor in repose, where he would be vulnerable.

The priests surrounded the unguarded city at evenly spaced intervals, and by the time the orb of day had cleared the highest of the hills, all was in readiness. While Blaht, the head priest, mumbled sacred incantations, his underlings held torches to the strange mixture in their urns. Dain, watching silently from the base of a hillock, saw blue strands of smoke curl upward, until the City of Necromancy, which had been bathed in early morning sunlight, became shrouded in darkness as billowing black clouds blotted the warm rays. The names of Doj and Bao were intoned continuously, and with each repetition the voices of the priests grew louder, until the eerie crescendo stirred scores of slumbering acolytes, who lay along the base of the walls. They rose unsteadily to their feet, and when they absorbed the scene around them they became terrified. They pounded frantically on the gate to gain admission.

Suddenly a great thunder arose, and the ground beneath their feet trembled. Bolts of searing fire rained down upon the City of Necromancy, one striking a group of cowering acolytes at the wall and reducing them to charred bones and reeking flesh. From within the city loud wails arose, and the voices of the acolytes invoked the name of Sothor to save them from this holocaust. But the

16

sorcerer did not immediately appear, and the destruction loosed on the city continued to reduce its populace.

The heavy gate suddenly swung open, crushing a pair of acolytes to pulp against the stone wall. A gaunt, shadowy figure emerged from the city, and for the first time in years Dain saw his hated foe. Sothor espied the king immediately, and he began striding toward him, all but ignoring the pleading, clutching hands of the terrified acolytes as he passed. Thunderstrokes continued to pummel the earth around him, and more of his followers were charred beyond recognition; but no bolt touched the sorcerer's body. His hatred for Dain was revealed in the fire that pulsed from his malignant eyes.

"You *dare* to wreak destruction on the sanctuary of a son of Esh?" he shrieked. "Know this, Dain, you and your accursed gods: I, Sothor, who would have practiced the arts of my ancestors in peace, and would have been content to offer the knowledge to those who sought it, now swear to you that the fate of Shadzea is sealed! May it take a hundred, or even a thousand years, I will some day succeed in calling upon the minions of Esh to crawl up from their deepest pits of blackness and cover the land, until there are none left to stand before them. All shall suffer the wrath of the Dark Ones, until time itself is no more. Even death will not free you from this, for we will know where to find your mouldering soul. *You* most of all, Dain, shall suffer the vengeance of Esh!"

But the king stood his ground, and he did not cower before the evil threats of the sorcerer. As he passed between two of the chanting priests the enraged Sothor raised his gnarled fingers to the heavens, and the pair fell to the loam, where they shriveled into black dust. With this atrocity Dain stepped forward, until he stood at

17

Blaht's elbow. The head priest fumbled in his robes for a moment, finally withdrawing a flat box covered in red velvet. He lifted the box ceremoniously above his head, and, after mumbling something unintelligible, he handed the contents to Dain. Around his neck the Survivor hung a long silver chain, at the end of which depended a large, gaudy amulet. He began to walk purposefully toward Sothor, and when the sorcerer espied the amulet he halted, his bony legs now unsteady. He knew that he had been defeated.

"*The Stone of Bao!*" he gasped as he stared at the blazing red jewel that highlighted the amulet. "I—I thought it to be lost these hundreds of years! Where did you find it?"

But Dain did not break his silence, and as he drew nearer the sorcerer cringed. Weakened by the night's obscene activities, Sothor struggled to summon the powers of Esh for one last futile defense. He staggered to his feet and thrust his hands toward Dain, and the king saw thin jets of searing flame emanate from the sorcerer's palms. But the Stone of Bao absorbed the brunt of this meager offering, while the remnants of the energy were reversed. Sothor was struck in one leg, this causing him excruciating pain. As he writhed on the ground, his acolytes rushed forward to help him. It was then that all heard Dain speak:

"You, Sothor, and your followers are banished forever from Shadzea. You will go to the great northern forest, farther even, if indeed anything exists beyond it. This is the closest you will ever come to our land. Doj and Bao have shown you that the powers of Esh are no match for them. The Stone of Bao will protect us from the likes of you forever. Now go quickly! Leave your foul wares, for we shall destroy them!"

And Sothor was banished from Shadzea to the far northern forest, the ragged remains of his acolytes along with him. Now Dain would not dare question the powers of Doj and Bao, and he devoted his reign to them. For more than a year the red priests remained in the City of Necromancy, until they felt certain that the city was cleansed of its past foulness in the eyes of their gods. Dain redubbed it the City of Gods, and he chose to rule Shadzea from there, instead of the City of Kings. This caused much grumbling on the part of his advisors, though none dared challenge the will of the king. Dain, known to all his descendants as the Pious One, at first even refused to initiate the third Rite of the Twenty. But this the advisors would not stand for, since the preservation of Shadzea was at stake. After Dain's death the next survivor, quite unpious, left the City of Gods to the red priests and returned to the City of Kings. All have since ruled from there.

Yes, they would learn much, the current princes of Shadzea. They would learn about all the monarchs in the strong Shadzean chain, and they would some day judge for themselves who was the greatest. Those well versed in the history of the kingdom might have sung the praises of Kerno, the fourth Survivor, whose last Princes' Trial had taken him to the Forest of Sothor, the vast northern forest so renamed during the rule of Kerno's predecessor. It was said that the exiled sorcerer had rebuilt his City of Necromancy deep within the forbidden wood, that his acolytes were great in number. But Kerno performed his self-assigned task, the retrieving of the fur of a rare and deadly beast. This trial took him deep into

19

the Forest of Sothor, and he was a changed man when he emerged. He methodically destroyed five princes on the day of the Reckoning, and his rule was marked with many other notable feats. He died without ever revealing to anyone his experiences in the grim forest. No other would-be Survivor, through the rule of Ornon, had returned from his Trial of Death to this dark place.

The weakest of Shadzea's kings, as the princes would doubtless learn, was Nhob, the thirteenth Survivor, father of Ornon. Nhob was the only one who stood in the courtyard on the day of the Reckoning, all his half brothers having been killed by the end of the fourth Princes' Trial. He was slain by a woman in her bedchamber four years after the Mating Week, and Shadzea was governed by a regency council until the fourteenth Survivor could be determined. All feared that Nhob's weaknesses would be transmitted to his offspring, but none had counted on Ornon, the ninth son, and this prince did not disappoint them.

Those with vivid memories of the fourteenth Rite of the Twenty could recall few who doubted that Ornon would one day claim the throne. As a determined youth he had accounted for the "accidental" deaths of four other princes even before the second trial had come to pass. His Trial of Death had taken him through the dreaded Terven Marshes to the City of Rogues on a deadly mission, which he performed admirably. Prior to the day of the Reckoning he was able to seek out and destroy one of his two remaining half brothers, even though the latter had been deeply sequestered. The second one he dispatched during the final conflict, his whistling sword, seemingly imbued with a sentience of its own, carving his mountainous kin, who by right should have been a far more formidable opponent, into unrecognizable pieces. Some whispered among themselves that Ornon had employed ensorcellment to achieve this, for rumor had it that years earlier an acolyte of Sothor had found his way to the City of Kings, and into Ornon's confidence. But no one could prove this, and none dared make the accusation.

Upon assuming the throne, Ornon's first act was to gather the combined forces of the Shadzean army and march to the distant City of Fishers, where through the decades the people of this region had complained the loudest over the taxes required of them. It was rumored that these disgruntled subjects had aligned themselves with a large island nation far across the Telliun Ocean, that even now great galleys were arriving to disgorge more outlanders along Shadzea's coast. As Ornon saw it, this portended naught but ill for his kingdom, and he was determined to see it rectified.

The new king of Shadzea struck quickly; the leaders of the planned rebellion were executed in the public square, while the foreign invaders were locked in the holds of their ships. These were hauled out to sea and sunk, the helpless prisoners drowned like rats. A new governor was hand picked by Ornon, who then returned to the capital. Most of the people in the City of Fishers felt relieved that they had escaped with their lives.

A second threat to Shadzea's dominance occurred not long after. In an uncharacteristic move many thousands of the nomadic Fashaars, bloodthirsty devils from the scorching Desert of Craters, had crossed the Kobur River and laid siege to the City of Slaves. They denied egress from the city, and they commandeered all arriving caravans, killing both merchants and drivers. Their demands included all the wealth and the female slaves within the city, a price that, once starvation and despair dominated, would have to be met.

By good fortune, a merchant that the Fashaars thought to be dead was merely wounded. He lay silently on the ground all afternoon, not daring to breathe, not even able to cry out when a horse trod across his back. Long after dark he managed to steal a mount and ride to the nearest village, arriving on the verge of death. Another sped to the City of Kings to bear the message, and once more the legions were called. By the time they reached the City of Slaves the governor, now faced with a starving citizenry, was ready to meet the demands of the turbaned rogues. But Ornon would have none of this. His army denied the Fashaars any means of escape, and in a one-sided battle the nomads were routed. Those who surrendered were lined up with their hands tied, all save one, a minor seikh. Ornon called this worthy before him.

"You will return to your scum across the river," announced the king. "But before you depart you will see how Shadzea welcomes its desert neighbors. Tell the other seikhs that this will be the fate of any Fashaar who sets foot upon our soil again."

Upon his signal a hundred swords fell in a whistling arc, and a hundred Fashaars were beheaded. The fortunate seikh blanched at the sight of the melding geysers of blood that spurted from the stumps of those who had been his comrades, and he gagged uncontrollably at the feet of the unmoving king. When the carnage was completed the Fashaar rode away, and he did not look back. Ornon provided the city with enough supplies to sustain them until the caravans came, and he led his army back toward the City of Kings, leaving the beleaguered city to dispose of the dead in any way they saw fit.

Of such incidents was the legend of Ornon, the fourteenth Survivor, based on, as the princes of Shadzea, his own sons, would eventually come to learn.

They stood side by side in the courtyard on the day of the Relinquishment, the sons of Ornon, while behind each hovered the woman who had given him life. There were eighteen in all, one having died in infancy, a second having been hurled to his death by his deranged mother, who immediately killed herself. But even when their numbers dwindled to fourteen, and nine, and four, they would still be referred to collectively as the Twenty, for such was the tradition begun by Offow.

In front of the scrubbed, sullen princes, about ten paces, stood the stern mentors. Adhering to the age-old customs, each mother turned her son twice before shoving him gently toward the one who had been assigned to him. This ceremony was enacted with little or no emotion on the part of most, though even a casual observer could not have missed the antithetical performances on the parts of two. The mother of Buz, Ornon's first son, had practically shoved the scowling youth at his mentor in her haste to depart. This woman, still young and probably once beautiful, appeared haggard, her long hair unkempt, her eyes glazed. But the mother of Dulok, twentieth and last of the king's offspring, nearly betrayed herself by hesitating after she and her son parted, and it took all her strength of will to keep from releasing the flood of tears that welled in her soft eyes. Had those in the courtyard looked even closer they would have been appalled to note the similar mask of despair on the face of

23

the would-be Survivor.

Dulok and Buz; or perhaps Buz and Dulok, as befitting the order of their birth. More must surely be said of these two sons of Ornon, whose names would figure prominently in this chapter of Shadzea's long history.

CHAPTER TWO

A MOTIVE FOR VENGEANCE

Nearly nine years before the day of the Relinquishment, the woman who would eventually bear the first son waited impatiently in her bedchamber for the return of Ornon, who had been gone from the city for more than a month in preparation for the upcoming Mating Week. Ashmala had indeed been beautiful, a fact hardly overlooked by the king, who had bedded her often since bringing her to the palace from the City of Slaves two years previously. Ornon might have even loved the sultry goddess, though this was difficult to say, for his sullen demeanor was impenetrable, even in her presence.

Ashmala's place in the palace had been assured, ironically, by her position as a handmaiden to Ornon's queen. Otessea, who by the dictates of Shadzean tradition Ornon had selected in his eighteenth year, and whom he had wed after assuming the reign, was a shrewish woman, much despised by the king. Her own feelings toward him were not dissimilar. They had not shared a bed since their second year of marriage, when a child born of accident was sent to the City of Gods, as was the custom. Destined to a childless life, Otessea took solace in the wealth and power associated with her title, and she insisted that Ornon stay out of her sight as much as possible. The scowling king was more than pleased to oblige her.

On the night of his return from the long month of meditation in the nearby hills, Ornon hastened to the chamber of Ashmala. But at the door he hesitated, for he was still sworn to abstinence, and there was seldom a time that his lust for this provincial beauty could be even marginally satisfied. Then, unable to contain himself, he cast open the portal, and the barely clad Ashmala, at first startled, flung herself eagerly into his arms. Her darting tongue probed his own hungrily, while her slim fingers glided over his body in a manner that made his senses reel. Finally he shoved her from him none too gently, this the only way he knew to break free of the spell she cast.

At first Ashmala was nonplussed; but she quickly shrugged this off as she told Ornon excitedly: "Sire, I have news. I've been selected as one of the fifty for the Mating Week!"

The king nodded, and a hint of a smile creased his face. "For the first and only time our lovemaking will be sanctioned by all of Shadzea. Don't you find this amusing?"

But Ashmala did not answer; instead she hung her head, and Ornon could see that she pouted.

"What is wrong, woman?" he demanded. "Don't you wish to bear the seed of Ornon?"

She looked at him. "My sole wish is to bear your child, and I know that I would give you a son. But if he is born too late, he will be destroyed!"

Ornon nodded grimly. "Such are the laws of Shadzea."

Ashmala sighed. "Yes, and there is nothing that we can do. Yet on the other hand— Perhaps there is!"

"What do you mean?"

"Tonight!" she exclaimed. "You must plant your seed this very night, for my time is now! This will increase the chance of our son being one of the Twenty. I believe in my heart that I will bear you the fifteenth Survivor!"

"But this is unheard of!" Ornon bellowed. "By Shadzean edict I must abstain until the Mating Week commences. How can you—?"

Ashmala turned away disconsolately, and Ornon, exhibiting a weakness that would have astonished his people, could not bear to see his favored concubine like this.

"All right," he conceded. "We *will* do it this way!" Then, as an afterthought: "I too believe that the Survivor will emerge from your womb."

The dark-skinned beauty's face glowed, and she tore loose the remainder of her garments as she beckoned Ornon to her furs. That night, the most unpardonable sin ever committed by a Survivor was consummated.

Later that night Ashmala stretched sinuously upon her couch, and she smiled complacently as she pondered on all that had occurred. In the time that the king had been gone from the city a change had overcome Ashmala, and she became obsessed with the thought of bearing the fifteenth Survivor. Her oft-declared love for Ornon had been forgotten in light of the one great desire that now dominated her being. By deceit and seduction she had seen to it that she would be selected as one of the fifty. Now, four days before the start of the Mating Week, she already bore the seed of Ornon. Did it disturb her that by his action Ornon had risked everything? Did she understand that the traditions binding Shadzea through the centuries had been violated? Not at all, for to be the mother of the fifteenth Survivor was all that mattered, and she would resort to anything to see this insane goal achieved.

Daynea, the mother of Dulok, was a scullery servant in the palace of Ornon. Though pleasing to the eye, she was by no means beautiful. But this simple girl was possessed of a kindly nature, and she endeared herself to all who came in contact with her.

Daynea was one of the last to be chosen for the Mating Week, this on the recommendation of a superior to the council, and despite the good-natured teasing of her peers she took this unexpected honor in stride. On the next to last day of the Mating Week she was led to the king's chamber, where all was accomplished in great haste, Ornon not uttering as much as a word to the young servant. Shortly afterward she knew that she was with child, as were all but three of the fifty.

During the initial period of waiting Daynea thought little about the life being nurtured within her womb. But the rounder she grew, the more aware she became of the miracle now transpiring, and she was saddened to think that the child who would some day emerge might be taken from her and destroyed. As the months passed she fought vainly against these emotions, and only the looming specter of her responsibility to Shadzea enabled her to marginally shield her tormented mind from the appalling prospect.

The Birth of Princes began with the arrival of a fine, healthy babe, whom Ornon named Buz. Six days passed before the next birth, but after this they came in rapid succession. Eighteen would-be Survivors had been born by the time Daynea felt the first pains of labor, and the physician's chamber where they led her was filled with other women in more advanced stages. But the gods chose to smile on the good-hearted scullery servant, for with the sands dwindling she delivered a beautiful, strong-lunged infant, whom the king named Dulok. With the arrival of the twentieth son the Birth of Princes was declared at an end, and a new phase of the Rite of the Twenty was begun.

Shadzea's young princes and their mothers were assigned private chambers in a special wing of Ornon's palace, where until the day of the Relinquishment they would seldom see another face. This was a particularly distasteful prospect to Ashmala, who had loathed her time of childbearing, for now the source of her discomfort was to be in her constant care for eight years. Within days of being confined in the chamber with the screaming infant she began to question her selfish desires. On one occasion, after being awakened by its crying, she even tried to smother the infant; but she quickly regained her senses, and never again did she attempt such an act, for in spite of her loathing for Buz, her ambition remained the dominant force in her life.

Repeatedly shunning the strong bonds of his fore-bears, Ornon became a frequent nocturnal visitor to his lover's chamber. But Ashmala, still young and quite beautiful, was tormented by the thought of her growing withered before being freed of her obligation. As the months passed she became an unbearable shrew, not unlike Otessea, and Ornon ceased his visits before Buz had seen one year. For this Ashmala was glad; she did not care if she never saw him again.

Ashmala's influence over the child was evident from the beginning, for the young Buz developed into a bitter, cruel, distrusting child. To the servants he was the scourge of the Twenty, and they despised him for the many terrible pranks he perpetrated. Once he set fire to the cloak of a maid, severely disfiguring her. Another time, while hurling objects from the balcony to the courtyard below, he struck a soldier in the head, and it took all the skills of the Shadzean physicians to save his life. But a young maid was not so fortunate, for in a fit of rage she had struck Buz across the back of his head as he engaged in one of the many intricate tortures that he devised for the docile pets given him by Ashmala. For this unheard of act the sensitive girl met a horrible death in a forbidden room beneath the palace.

For years Ashmala poured her venom into Buz's impressionable ears, and as the day of the Relinquishment approached she knew that the seed was well planted. Now Buz would channel his hatred and cruelty into another direction, the ultimate destruction of his as yet unseen half brothers. Although too young to grasp the complexities of achieving the role and responsibilities of the Survivor, Buz nonetheless became enamored of the title, and the fact that these others were all that stood in his way made his loathing of them all the more profound. Ashmala was certain that this child, the first son of Ornon, would see her obsession fulfilled.

The eight years following the Birth of Princes were the most joyous of Daynea's young life. Ornon never once came to see his twentieth son, nor did Daynea care. Had she not nurtured Dulok within her womb? Had she not suckled him at her breast in his earliest, most helpless months? What interest could Ornon have in this child, other than to see it as a potential heir to his throne? No, this child belonged to Daynea, and she would share it with no one.

In the years that she spent with Dulok the kindly scullery servant poured out her love to him, the only thing in her life that she had ever called her own. And Dulok in turn grew to love the smiling face that he saw hover above him, the face of the one who fed him when he was hungry, and soothed him when he was ill; the face of the one who was always there, and who never spoke harshly to him.

Daynea knew all too well of the responsibility she bore, and the duties that she must perform. It grieved her to teach this loving child the evils of distrust and ambition, but she knew that, without preparation, his life past the age of eight would at best be tentative. She taught him all that he must know to survive, and in the final year Dulok understood. He swore to his mother that, in spite of who he was and what he must do, he would never forsake the qualities that she had instilled in him; that he would use these qualities to temper the hardness that would help him survive to the end, to the throne of Shadzea. And with the day of the Relinquishment near he vowed, to Daynea's ill-concealed joy, that he would not allow the stringent laws of Shadzea to prevent them from again seeing one another.

The day of the Relinquishment was waning; the tense, weary princes were led to their quarters by their respective mentors, most all men of dedication and ambition, for to be mentor to the Survivor meant a position of power and wealth in later years. The quarters

31

of the Twenty, located in a spacious chamber on the lower level, were easily accessible from the courtyard through a large oak door. Along one wall of the sparsely furnished hall were nine utilitarian bunks, each with an upper berth. On the opposite wall were individual cots for the mentors, who would seldom be far from the side of their charges.

That night, the first the princes shared together, all within the chamber were awakened by a commotion. With torches lit the mentors hurried to the source, and they saw what had occurred: the second son, Kerlis, lay dead in a pool of gore, his skull smashed open on the stone floor. He had occupied the bunk atop Buz, who expressed his astonishment at the tragedy that had occurred so near to him. He recalled how only hours before he had overheard Kerlis grumbling about the height of the bed, and how he would have preferred a lower one. Buz had decided to offer Kerlis his own bed the very next day, but now it would not matter. The body was removed, and no further word was said regarding the accident. However, Buz slept alone from that day forth.

The rigid daily activity of the Twenty varied little for the next two years. The princes rose early, bathed themselves, and dined on rough but nourishing fare. For the rest of the morning each was sequestered with his mentor in a confining cubicle. Here, these sages sought to impart their wisdom and knowledge to the would-be rulers. They were first taught to read and write. They then learned of the history and geography of their land; of mathematics and science. They were told of the ultimate good, represented in the unseen images of Doj and Bao, and of their antitheses, the Dark Ones of foul Esh. The expulsion of Sothor from Shadzea, and the unspeakable horrors to be found in the northern forest, were also related. The mentors, most of whom believed the legends of Sothor to be mere whimsey, nonetheless carried out the traditions of the ancestors. Yet even the most mature of their charges suffered his share of nightmares at the thought of such horror.

After the midday meal the Twenty spent an hour in the courtyard pond, where they were allowed to swim and play freely. Interaction was acceptable, though this usually resulted in fighting, which caused the mentors to scrutinize their charges more closely. Wyak, the tenth son, was nearly drowned in such an encounter, but his mentor pumped the water from his lungs, and he survived, at least for the time being.

The rest of the afternoon was spent with the finest soldiers in service to Ornon, who would demonstrate the use of weapons to the Twenty. Accuracy with the longbow, as well as proficiency with the sword and lance, were stressed. The princes became quite capable in weaponry, but none quite so much as Dulok, Buz, and Korb, the seventh son. Although noncontact was the rule, Buz took pleasure in inflicting small, painful wounds on those he engaged. Soon all refused to cross blades with him, all save Dulok, and as the twentieth son parried the thrusts and slashes of Buz with deftness and ease, the earliest seeds of hatred were sown. Buz despised all of his half brothers, but in Dulok he saw a definite obstacle to his goal. Something in the cruel eyes of the first son warned Dulok that from then on he'd best be wary.

When the evening meal was finished the Twenty were once again sequestered with their mentors, this time to review what they had learned earlier. It behooved them to absorb their lessons well, for if the mentor was satisfied with his pupil's aptitude for that day he would dismiss him early. Until the ninth hour, when all would retire, the fortunate princes could partake of some free time within the boundaries of their domain, which consisted of their quarters and the courtyard. Many refined their skills with the bow, some read, while others used the time for extra sleep. The area was guarded heavily; none could enter, nor could any of the Twenty leave the confines of their narrow world.

Thus went the rigid early life of the Twenty. Their time was controlled and scrutinized every moment of the day, whether asleep or awake. For the first two years Dulok found it impossible to keep the promise he had made to his mother before they parted. But during the third year, a series of events prodded the sharp witted youth into action. Bigor, who slept below Dulok, had fallen victim to an errant arrow in the courtyard one day. None had witnessed the source of the missile, though most harbored their own suspicions. Dulok now occupied the lower bunk, which was the one closest to the courtyard door. No one took the vacated upper bunk.

Other events occurred almost simultaneously with this. The king's guard, so numerous at the beginning, had been reduced, this owing to the growth and responsibility of the princes. None stood by their door, while only two were perched atop the wall overlooking the courtyard, and much of the time they watched the road that led to the palace. The mentors, confined continually with their charges from the first, were now allowed three hours of leisure time twice in seven days, between the ninth and twelfth hours. Only two were required to remain in the princes' quarters on a given night.

One evening, not long past the ninth hour, Dulok lay awake upon his cot, restless, and listened to the sounds of sleep that echoed softly through the chamber. It had been a particularly demanding day, and all were exhausted. But Dulok was unable to sleep, for the thought of the kindly woman who toiled without hope in the scullery was more than he could bear. The two mentors in the chamber that night were both at the far end, and by the dim torch light Dulok could tell that each slumbered deeply. After rearranging his sleeping furs to give the appearance of a body in repose, he rose to his feet and glided noiselessly to the door. He opened it just enough to allow his lithe body egress, and with a reassuring glance to his rear he edged silently into the courtyard.

Dulok first noted the position of the guards, neither of whom were looking into the courtyard at the moment. The door that led into the main building was directly opposite him, and he could have reached it quickly by crossing the courtyard, but he dared not take the chance. With his back against the wall he circled the yard, always remaining in the shadows. In this manner he reached the door, and he promptly vanished inside.

Daynea had once mentioned the location of the scullery, and the perceptive youth was able to find his way there, even through the confusing maze of passageways. Twice he encountered others, but he easily concealed himself. He discovered the large kitchen and walked boldly across it, for at this late hour it was deserted. In the adjoining scullery he also saw no one, nor had he expected to. His interest was focused on the closed door against the far wall, the one that led into a small cubicle. He traversed the floor in great haste and slowly opened the portal.

Daynea, only half asleep, heard the slight creaking. She raised herself to a sitting position, instantly alert.

"Who—who is it?" she asked timidly as the door continued to open. "What do you—*Dulok! Thank the gods!*"

Daynea leaped to her feet, while the youth swung open the door and ran to the ecstatic woman. She tearfully embraced her dear son, and the pain of the previous years was instantly dismissed. Thus were they reunited, until more than an hour had passed, and he was forced to return to the unwanted life predestined for him.

Months passed, and the routine of the Twenty changed little. But Dulok was happy, for at least one night in five he spent an hour or two with the kindly woman who had given him life, and love. Dulok swore that some day he would take her away from the City of Kings, perhaps to some isolated province, where they could begin a new life. Daynea chided him for such talk, for he was a son of Ornon, and his responsibility was immense. But inwardly she thrilled at the prospect, and she prayed that some day it would come to pass.

One night, as he strode the corridor on his way to another rendezvous with Daynea, Dulok felt a strange prickling sensation on the back of his neck. He wheeled about quickly, certain that he was being followed, but the passageway was still. On he went, but the feeling did not leave him. He had never encountered it before, and it was troubling. His own safety was of no concern, but he feared for the well-being of the innocent woman in the scullery, for he knew that what they did was forbidden by Shadzean law. However, he met with no difficulty, and he was much relieved.

Five nights later, the twentieth son of the Shadzean king sat in the small cubicle opposite his mother, and together they discussed the future. Daynea knew that her strong-willed son meant to keep his promise, and she now shared fully in his great excitement. He had told her that their time of flight from the City of Kings would be soon.

Suddenly the door burst open, and the dream vanished. In the doorway stood Ornon, and at his right hand a leering Buz. Two armed guards followed in their wake.

"You see, Sire, it is as I told you," said Buz venomously. "I became suspicious weeks ago, when I saw him moving about long after the ninth hour. Last time I followed him, and he came here, to rest at the bosom of the low scum that bore him. He is weak, unfit to be the Survivor, and he should be destroyed!"

"Silence!" Ornon snapped. "*I* will decide what must be done here. But you can be assured that Dulok will suffer greatly for this. Guards!"

The two soldiers entered the small room, each grabbing one of Dulok's arms. The young prince struggled vainly, while Daynea stood against the back wall, her body trembling. Ornon relieved one of the guards of his sword, and, while Buz shrieked with maniacal glee, the cold monarch silently drove the sharpened tip into the bosom of Daynea. The metal pierced her heart, and with a soft moan she slumped to the hard floor.

Buz immediately faced Dulok, and he would have reveled in seeing the heartbroken youth cry out in anguish. But Dulok would not allow him the pleasure. He ceased his struggles, and his face became frozen in a mask of grim determination. To his other half brothers he had been indifferent, while Buz he had always disliked for his cruelty. Now that feeling had grown into intense hatred, not only for Buz but for Ornon, his own father! On that terrible night, months before his eleventh year had ended, his destiny became clear: he would survive at all cost, so that he might stand on the day of the Reckoning. Should Buz survive to that day he would destroy him mercilessly, though not before prolonging the vile prince's torment. He would then be proclaimed the fifteenth Survivor, and Ornon would approach him for the symbolic embrace. But he would find no grateful heir awaiting him. Instead, he would meet a death even more terrible than that of his first son. Only then would the debt be satisfied for the cruel and cowardly act of violence perpetrated that night in the scullery.

Only then would the life of the gentle Daynea be avenged.

CHAPTER THREE

THE EARLY PRINCES' TRIALS

The rigorous training of the Twenty continued, and each year it became more intense. Horsemanship was added to the curriculum, and the young princes reveled in this, not only for their love of riding but for the opportunity it afforded them to leave the confines of their world. Every second day they were escorted to a large stable north of the palace. For all it was the first time they had seen the splendid City of Kings, and they were awed as they realized that all of this could be theirs. The determination that held each one in its grip grew considerably.

Dulok and Buz never spoke to one another, though the animosity that existed between the two could be sensed by the rest. They avoided contact during mock battles, lest one of them forget himself and inflict injury, perhaps even death, upon the other. Not even a son of Ornon could perform such an act, if witnessed by others, with impunity. That prince would be taken from the Twenty, and his chance of becoming Survivor would be gone.

Dulok, following the death of Daynea, renewed his

training vigorously. He excelled at everything he attempted, and his zeal was such that he constantly strove to outdo himself. This new attitude pleased Qual, his mentor, for until then he considered his charge to be lacking in desire. He now saw Dulok's potential being realized, and for the first time since taking the youth under his wing he firmly believed that the attainment of Survivor was realistically within reach. For himself it was a matter of pride, for he was older than the other mentors, and cared little for wealth or power. He would be quite old if his charge survived to the day of the Reckoning.

The fourteenth year came to an end for the Twenty, and the time for the first Princes' Trial was at hand. The ranks of the princes had continued to diminish, the latest victim being Igol, the thirteenth son. He had succumbed to numerous wounds inflicted during an active session of swordplay, and no one prince in particular could shoulder the blame, although one deep, deadly gash had been discovered in Igol's side. Fifteen determined youths were now left to face the initial ordeal.

Ornon and his council were on hand to see the princes off on the day they left with their mentors for Lake Porsat. Dulok stared maliciously at his hated sire, but Ornon chose not to gaze upon his twentieth son. He looked instead at Buz, and only one without sight could have missed the admiration in the half-smile that cracked the hard face of the ruthless monarch. Another unpardonable sin had been cast upon Ornon's growing cairn, for it was evident to all who were there that the Shadzean king had already chosen his successor. All knew that his personal feelings did not matter, since prowess was the only way to attainment. And yet—they wondered if this was really so.

The road to Lake Porsat, if indeed one could call what they traveled upon a road, was long, but uneventful. Even the well organized provincial bandits shunned the caravan, for the Shadzean guard were many, and the potential plunder limited. The party spent one night in the City of Artisans, but otherwise they encountered little of civilization, save for a few small farming or mining villages.

Lake Porsat, a vast body of water, was the first of its kind ever seen by the princes. Although they had learned much regarding this lake, as well as the Telliun Ocean to the west, all were astonished at the sight. The permanent galley for the first trial, used only fourteen times in the hundreds of years since Boga first set foot upon it, was tied tightly to the shore with a heavy length of hemp. The grizzled caretaker, forewarned of the caravan's arrival, had scrubbed and polished the vessel, and it glistened like a jewel as it floated upon the shimmering lake surface.

The Shadzean guards now turned into oarsmen, and the small, sleek craft shot across the lake with its valuable cargo. For more than an hour they rowed, stopping only after a signal from the caretaker. The instructions were then read, traditionally, by the mentor of the first son, an intelligent but heartless man named Lonz.

"Princes of Shadzea, hear and obey!" he roared. "You of the Twenty who have survived the first fourteen years of your lives have come to Lake Porsat, and here, on this day, you will endure the first, and surely the least difficult, of the Princes' Trials. You will swim to the bottom of the lake, there to retrieve a porsat blossom, with which you will return to the galley. Remember this, however: all excursions preceding this one have resulted

41

in at least one death. In your minds you will convince yourselves that this will not happen to you. Survival is Life; Life is Survival!"

The ceremony over, Lonz rejoined the mentors near the bow. The fifteen somber youths, each clad only in a breechcloth, lined the sides of the galley and awaited their signal. Lonz raised a large, blunt mallet high above his head, and after assuring himself the lads were prepared he brought it down upon a wide, leather-bound drum. The echo of the heavy thud across the lake had scarcely died when the last of the youths disappeared beneath the surface. If tradition could be thought an appropriate indicator, there were surely some who had breathed their last.

Dulok, a strong swimmer, sliced downward through the murky water, accidently brushing against one of his half brothers in his haste. The other youth, fearful of attack, wheeled to defend himself, but Dulok merely pulled away and continued his descent. The lake bottom, although deep, was within reach, and Dulok shortly found himself on the stony floor. It took but a matter of moments to locate and pluck a brilliant porsat blossom from amidst the undulating foliage. He doubted if any would encounter much difficulty.

As he started for the surface, he saw that some of the others were on the lake floor. He was sure that all must be there by now, but he could not see them through the murk. There was one, however, who was all too clear to him: the hated Buz. The first son did not notice Dulok, and he therefore believed that the action he was about to perpetrate would go unnoticed. Dulok saw that in one hand Buz carried a porsat blossom, while in the other he bore a fist-sized rock. He was stealthily approaching an unsuspecting victim, whom Dulok recognized as Vassoe, the twelfth son. Dulok was helpless in the watery environment, and could not warn his doomed half brother. He saw the rock cave in Vassoe's skull, and he watched as the twelfth son sank limply to the foliage below.

Buz dropped the rock and struck out for the surface; but as an afterthought he turned, and when he saw Dulok he realized that his act had been witnessed. He knew what implications this bore, and he believed that his only chance would be to destroy Dulok. But his recent efforts had all but expended the air in his lungs, and he knew that he could not remain below any longer. With a vicious scowl he began ascending to the galley, resolved to deny any accusations that Dulok might choose to make. The twentieth son, sickened by the cowardly actions of his half brother, set out after him.

Buz had already presented the porsat blossom to the mentors, and was drying himself, when Dulok climbed over the galley railing. The first son glared at him, but Dulok chose not to gaze upon the despised countenance. Instead, he too gave the prize to the mentors, and then he began to dress.

Thirteen of the princes had successfully passed the first trial, and now they, along with their mentors, lined the deck of the galley to await the other two. But many minutes passed, and neither appeared. After a grim nod of agreement from the majority of the mentors, Lonz again struck the large drum.

"The first of the Princes' Trials is over!" he announced formally. "All those now aboard have been successful. Two more of the Twenty have fallen from the ranks. As has been the custom since the days of Offow, an inquiry must be made into their assumed deaths. The two that have not returned are Vhog, the fourth son, and Vassoe, the twelfth son. Can any of those present enlighten us as to their fate?"

"I know of the fate of Vhog!" shouted Robbik, the third son. All eyes turned toward him. "I saw him at the bottom of the lake, his foot wedged tightly between jagged rocks. Naturally I swam to assist him, but his efforts had expended his breath, and he was dead when I reached him."

Most of the princes smiled inwardly. They did not doubt that Vhog had met such a fate, but they were certain that Robbik's professed attempts at aid were not made in any haste.

Lonz nodded thoughtfully at the third son. "The death of Vhog is duly noted, and the record is closed. Now, what of Vassoe? Does anyone know of Vassoe?"

The young princes stared blankly at one another, all save Buz, who glared venomously at Dulok. He had practiced his defense a dozen times since surfacing, and he was prepared to offer it emphatically. But, much to the amazement of Buz, the twentieth son chose to remain silent. Buz could not conceive of Dulok's reason for this, except—yes, that must be it! Dulok arrived seconds after the dispatching of Vassoe, and therefore did not witness the murder! A slight smile creased his twisted face, and he relaxed.

But Dulok had not suddenly lost his tongue. To incriminate Buz now would hardly satisfy his lust for vengeance. He had other things in mind for the young devil, and only on the day of the Reckoning would his revenge be consummated. He had decided, even before surfacing, to let Buz live for the time being.

For long minutes the hard eyes of Lonz went from face to face, until the princes fidgeted nervously under the cold stare. "Your silence tells me that no one witnessed the fate of Vassoe," he stated suspiciously. "So be it! Vassoe's death shall be noted as a drowning, and the record will be closed. Caretaker! Point the bow toward land, and let us return."

The galley was rowed back to the shore, there to await its next voyage some thirty-five years hence. The princes and their mentors returned to the City of Kings, where Ornon was informed of the outcome. The first Princes' Trial had passed, and for most it was quickly forgotten.

Three more years passed, and the training of the Twenty did not abate, not even for a day. The princes were now more aware of the necessity for survival, and none lost their lives during that time, although Behus, the sixth son, was severely injured in a fall from a horse. He eventually recovered, but he found himself far behind his half brothers in training, and it was unlikely that he could ever make this up.

By the time of the second Princes' Trial each youth had grown considerably, for full manhood was nearly upon them. There were few among the Shadzean guards who could match any of the princes in horsemanship and weaponry, so skilled had each become. The nature of the second trial, though unknown to them, would certainly be designed to test these skills to the fullest. Many of them looked toward this challenge with apprehension.

Once again Ornon saw his sons leave the city; but this time, heeding the advice of his council, he did not single any one out. Buz tried in vain to catch his father's eye, but Ornon gazed impassively at the caravan in general.

His feelings regarding his first son had not changed, but Buz could not know of this, and he sulked for most of the journey.

The princes and their mentors, again surrounded by a large escort, rode south on a journey that seemed never to end. The rugged terrain of the southern provinces slowed them considerably, and on some days they were able to advance only a few leagues. One guard was killed when his mount, upon sighting a small serpent, reared and threw him. Another guard lost his life when his horse stumbled upon a narrow hill trail that they were climbing. Both fell to the jagged rocks below.

After much adversity the caravan arrived at the foot of the Torrean Mountains, the forboding peaks that marked the southern boundary of Shadzea. Only the day before they had encountered Ornon's border guards, who were glad for the chance to welcome others. Their life at this bleak outpost was one of boredom, for never did they see even the hint of a potential enemy. They were certain that nothing existed beyond the Torrean Mountains, but they were merely soldiers, sworn to follow the orders of the king. Such an outpost had been maintained since the time of Boga.

The princes of Shadzea were each equipped with a length of rope and a grappling hook. These, along with their knife, longsword, and some meager stores, were all they would take with them. Once again, this time in the shadow of the stone titans, all listened to the words of Lonz:

"Princes of Shadzea, hear and obey!" he began ceremoniously. "You of the Twenty that have survived the first seventeen years of your lives have come to the Torrean Mountains, and here, beginning this day, you

46

will endure the second of the Princes' Trials. You will climb high into the mountains, there to retrieve the feather of a scarlet hawk. This creature makes its aerie atop the loftiest of peaks, and you can be sure that adversity will ascend with you before one is found. Even then, you'll quickly learn that the hawk is among the most formidable of foes. He will not freely relinquish his plumage. Remember that all past excursions here have resulted in manifold deaths. In your minds you will convince yourselves that this will not happen to you. Survival is Life; Life is Survival!"

The ritual concluded, the princes were taken to their respective sites of departure, each one more than a mile from that of another. This was done to lessen any chance of foul play between competitors on the isolated peaks. That they were interspersed by order of birth eliminated any possible meeting between Dulok and Buz. To Dulok it mattered little; but the first son, who would have been glad for any opportunity to destroy his adversary, swore silently at the fates.

Thus began the assault on the Torrean Mountains by the Twenty, those who remained. As befitting their bloodline they ascended calmly, their heads high, their eyes alert for any would-be dangers. None had uttered a sound when the nature of the trial was recited, but all knew, more so now than ever before, that the attainment of Survivor was no longer a game. Each stood an even chance of losing his life in the quest for the feather of a scarlet hawk, and each resolved to overcome the obstacles with grim determination.

For the first hour the path that Buz followed sloped upward gradually, and the first son found no difficulty in ascending, save for the thorny shrubs that tore at his legs. But soon the incline grew steeper, the brambles thicker. To cover each yard required greater effort, and the bleeding prince swore lustily in disgust. When he finally topped a ridge he saw that his trial was about to worsen, for his way to the top was impeded by immense boulders and sheer precipices. His peers would have felt amusement, the mentors shame, to know of his terror as he stared at the towering peaks. But he carried the blood of Ornon, the blood of many Survivors before him, and he knew what he must do. Slowly, fearfully, he began his assault of the threatening mountain.

On two occasions did the quest of Buz nearly end, and each time he imagined himself being dashed to a bloody death on the rocks below. But fortune, as well as a sturdy rope, was with him, and after hours of hazardous climbing he hauled himself onto a narrow plateau. He slumped to the ground, exhausted, and he partook of the minimal amount of water that had been allowed each prince. As he drank he gazed upward, and what he saw made him gasp. He had thought much of the hard climbing to be over, but the lofty pinnacles that reared their heads so high as to disappear in the dense clouds above assured him otherwise. He had scaled but a fraction of the mountain, and the worst of it lay before him. His head drooped to his knees, and he moaned as the realization that he might not survive the second Princes' Trial struck him.

The silence of the hills was suddenly shattered by a blood-chilling screech. Buz leaped to his feet, his fatigue temporarily forgotten, his sword extended. At the far end of the plateau, near the foot of a huge, isolated boulder, was a creature, the source of the terrible sound. Lonz, his mentor, had often described such a thing, but not until learning the nature of the second trial did Buz believe he would ever have cause to see one. The fiery red feathers, the piercing eyes, the ferocious beak and the deadly talons left no doubt: the beast was the fearsome scarlet hawk of the Torrean Mountains.

The sight of the formidable bird, whose wingspread measured nearly twenty feet across, caused Buz to shudder. At first he retreated slowly, and only a hasty glance behind prevented him from taking the final step that would have plunged him to a bloody death. He eyed the hawk cautiously, his sword still poised. He expected that the great bird would raise itself in the air at any moment and attack him, but it did not. Instead it continued to scream, and Buz saw that it thrashed wildly on the hard ground. Emboldened, he approached the bird. As he did he chanced a quick glance upward, and from what he saw he pieced together the story.

High above his head, on the side of a sheer facing, the first son of Ornon saw a crimson stain. This hawk had apparently been blinded, by what only Doj knows, and had flown into the cliff at great speed. It had plummeted downward, where it now lay. The thrashing and screeching were part of its rite of death, and the proud creature was relinquishing life begrudgingly.

Buz smiled as he realized his good fortune. His quest would end right here, and he would be forced to risk his life no further. His debased soul would not allow him to see this act as cowardly. Instead, he accepted it as a sign from the gods. They had sent this bird to him, for they knew that the title of Survivor would be his by right, and they saw no additional reason for him to continue. Yes, he was certain that such was the case.

He moved forward to dispatch the scarlet hawk, but

the fierce creature summoned whatever strength it still possessed in an effort to defend itself. It rose unsteadily on one claw, and its wicked beak snapped menacingly at the intruder. Buz, exercising discretion, decided to await the imminent demise of the bird. He built a tiny fire on the plateau, for the sun had already vanished beyond the rim, and it was cold at this higher elevation.

Within the hour the final shriek of the noble bird echoed through the range. By the meager light of his fire Buz could see the scarlet body rise in one last, convulsive shudder. Now it lay rigid in death. Buz casually strode to it and plucked it clean of feathers, the finest of which he stuffed in his belt. He then roasted the hawk over his small fire and devoured part of it, for he was famished. He settled in for the night, knowing that he would spend at least two days on this snug plateau, for none below would expect him any sooner.

Dulok did not encounter such good fortune as Buz, nor would he have taken advantage of it if he had. His ascent was arduous, and by sunset of the first day he had negotiated only half of his peak. He spent the night on a narrow ledge, and he nearly froze, for there was no room to light a fire. His only luck was in the dearth of wind, which, had it not chilled him further, would surely have toppled him from his dangerous perch.

He continued his climb the next morning at the first hint of light. The rest of the mountain was fraught with hazards too numerous to mention. Suffice it to say that by mid-afternoon Dulok was near the summit, and aside from assorted cuts and bruises he was little the worse for wear. But still he had not found any aeries, and he wondered at this, for he was certain that he was at a sufficient elevation.

A narrow precipice hung overhead, and with the aid of his grappling hook he was able to haul himself atop it. Once on the plateau he pulled his rope up after him. He turned, and what he observed made him forget, at least for the moment, his reason for being there. From where he stood, he had an unobstructed view of the land beyond the Torrean Mountains to the south. Even the many clouds, above which he had climbed, did not inhibit the sight. He saw glistening rivers, lush, fertile fields, green valleys. To him it appeared as if in a dream, contrasting greatly with the harshness of the Shadzean landscape. Surely there was much to be seen there; strange beasts, and perhaps—even stranger people. This land of mystery beckoned enticingly, and the desire to explore the world beyond the Torrean Mountains overwhelmed him. But he quickly remembered who he was, and most of all he remembered Daynea. Such a frivolous undertaking would have to wait.

A loud whooshing sound to his rear suddenly snapped Dulok from his reverie. In a lightning movement he drew his sword and whirled around to face the source of the distraction. Hovering above the ground, only yards from him, was a huge scarlet hawk. He had been told of this bird by Qual, but still he was not prepared for such an awesome sight. The bird screeched menacingly, and in an instant Dulok understood the reason for its agitation. Behind the hawk, in the center of the plateau, was a large nest, in which were three eggs. Dulok had not noticed it at first, so intent was he on his discovery. Now he realized that the angry hawk would surely attack, for this intruder represented a danger to its unhatched young.

With a loud beating of wings the fiery engine of

destruction dove at Dulok, and to the young prince it was as if a red demon, drawn from the darkest recesses of a deranged mind, had chosen to vent its fury on him. He flattened himself to the ground as the creature passed over him, but still it managed to rake flesh from his back with its deadly talons. Twice, three times it swooped down on him, and soon his waistcoat had been turned into bloody rags. On one pass he attempted to injure the beast with his sword, but in a vicious foray the hawk struck the weapon from his hand, and it flew out of reach.

The scarlet hawk now lit on Dulok, and it proceeded to gouge him with its razorlike beak. Dulok, struggling desperately, managed to keep his face turned away from the creature, lest it tear his eyes from their sockets. Then, utilizing his considerable strength, the young prince grabbed the hawk tightly around its thick neck, this despite his numerous injuries. Now the advantage belonged to the twentieth son, and with a vicelike grip he began to squeeze the life from his erstwhile attacker. The hawk, with a spark of understanding aglow in its tiny brain, thrashed madly, as if it wished to lift its executioner off the ground. But the determined young man would not relinquish his death hold, and after a few more vain attempts the great bird expired.

Minutes passed before Dulok rose slowly to his feet, for his efforts, as well as the loss of blood, had weakened him. He discarded the remains of his tattered waistcoat, for it was less than useless. Pouring out a minimal amount of his precious water, he bathed his numerous wounds as best he could. After retrieving his sword he returned to the dead bird and gazed upon it. The scarlet hawk was a beautiful creature, and it seemed a waste to have to destroy it. But it was not his role to question, for he was a son of Ornon, and he knew what was required of him. He leaned over and ceremoniously plucked a large feather from the bird. He then began his descent from the plateau, not even daring another look at the land beyond the Torrean Mountains. He knew that the hawk he had killed would have a mate, that it would eventually return to the nest. The young prince had neither the desire nor the strength to do battle with another of these mountain monarchs.

That night, upon a narrow ledge, Dulok managed to light a tiny fire, without which he would have frozen. Even the meager protection offered him by his scanty waistcoat was gone. His descent to that ledge had been hampered greatly by his wounds, many of which had reopened as they were scraped along the rocks. A physician had accompanied the party to the Torrean Mountains, and he now awaited the princes at the base camp. Dulok called upon Doj and Bao to see him safely to the camp, where the much needed care could be administered.

His dreams were troubled, his sleep restless, and in the dark hours he awoke with a start. His hand gripped the hilt of his sword tightly, until his knuckles turned white. In his state of half sleep he knew not what he would defend himself against, for his dreams had brought him foes unlike the great hawk that he had destroyed, unlike anything ever known to him. He saw beasts that were serpents, but then were not. Slimy, misshapen creatures haunted him, some with humanlike appendages. Huge leviathans rose from the murky depths of foul, polluted lakes to crawl up on the shore and contaminate the earth with their vile droppings. What unknown power could have sent him these accursed visions? He, a prince of

Shadzea, knew little of such things. Only the minds of those who dwelt in the unspeakable Forest of Sothor could conceive of such horrors. What link bound him to that place, surely the gateway to the black depths of Esh?

The disturbed youth found the thought of any additional sleep to be repulsive, but fatigue and injury proved greater forces, and reluctantly he succumbed. Through the remainder of that night the gods were with him, for he slept a deep, dreamless sleep. At the earliest hint of dawn he awoke, and, though quite sore, found himself to be refreshed. With renewed spirits he continued his descent, arriving at the base camp after midday. The relieved Qual was the first to greet him. After presenting the scarlet hawk's feather to the mentors, he hastened to the physician's tent for much needed attention.

While the physician soothed Dulok's wounds with a foul smelling balm, Qual advised him that he was as yet only the third prince to return with the prized feather. Esaaz, the eighth son, had returned the previous day, while Ulus, the sixteenth, had arrived only that morning. Esaaz had been virtually unscathed, while Ulus' wounds, although serious, would heal. Dulok absorbed this information silently, and when the ministrations of the physician were completed, he retired. For Dulok, the second Princes' Trial had ended.

The intense watch kept by the mentors continued. The next day three more princes reached the base camp: Robbik, the third son; Skoj, the fifth son; Xonik, the fourteenth son. The following day brought Cravik, the eighteenth son, and, amidst Dulok's mixed emotions, the despised Buz. The next saw the appearance of Korb, the seventh son, and, within hours, Wyak, the tenth. Wyak appeared to be in the worst condition of those who returned, for he had barely made it off the mountain. Only minutes after presenting his feather to the mentors, he died. No prince mourned his passing, though all admired his courage.

Though the Shadzeans remained in their camp at the foot of the Torrean Mountains for seven more days, no additional princes appeared. Lonz ceremoniously called an end to the second Princes' Trial, and the caravan began its lengthy trek back to the City of Kings. Ornon would see nine of his sons, but four would call the Torrean Mountains their final place of rest. Left there with Wyak were Behus, the sixth son, Roffol, the fifteenth son, and Botus, the seventeenth. The age-old Rite of the Twenty had reduced the ranks of the princes to less than half by subjecting them to unspeakable dangers and hardships. But for those who survived, there was worse still to come.

CHAPTER FOUR

SALLIA

From the time of the First Rite of the Twenty, all of Shadzea's figurehead queens had been chosen from among the daughters of the king's advisors. But fortune had not smiled on the Shadzean council in the reign of Ornon, for during the period of two years that began with the Mating Week, only four daughters had been born to this nobility. One succumbed in its infancy, leaving three to stand on the brink of womanhood by the end of the princes' eighteenth year.

Dhela was a spoiled girl whose looks pleased everyone, especially herself. But her vanity stood a distant second to her ambition, which had been instilled in her from the earliest dawn of understanding by her mother. She knew what she was being groomed for, and she was determined to achieve it by any means possible. That she was taken under the wing of Otessea served to inflate her already swelled ego. In this girl Otessea saw herself as she once was, and she understood the girl's motivations. Dhela represented a worthy successor to the queen.

Ciren, though far from beautiful, was not an unattractive girl. But from the beginning all could tell that there was something different about her. At times she was gentle and kind, and she would warm the hearts of those around her. Then, without warning, she would fly into rage, and she would seem more terrible than a wounded Shadzean plains bull. She would hurl things at anyone who had the misfortune to stray within her sphere, whether parent or otherwise. Just as suddenly she would change again, and the incident would be forgotten. Many believed that the responsibility she bore weighed heavily upon her and caused this malady, that maturity would temper these fits. Regardless of this, she made life unbearable for those around her, especially the many playmates who were forced to share in her unpredictable days.

Sallia, the third of the daughters born to the council, was quite unlike her peers. Though little more than comely, she nevertheless radiated a beauty from within that endeared her to those who knew her. Her warm eyes glowed with an understanding of life that far surpassed her young years. She also knew of her destiny, but the knowledge saddened her at best, for she cared little for such matters. She avoided Dhela and Ciren as much as possible, for both were cruel to her. Dhela would especially chide her for her lack of ambition, and would taunt her with promises of things she would do when she became queen of Shadzea. Sallia would choose the simple children of the servants as playmates over these two.

But Sallia also found much joy in solitude. She would stroll in the garden of the palace for hours, with only the flowers and the insects as her company. She loved the tiny animals that lived in the trees, and the brightly colored birds that nested there. While alone, she would think much about her future, and she prayed that she would not be the choice of the Survivor. Much of the time she was able to convince herself that none but Dhela could be destined for such a position, but she knew that this was no assurance. At such times she would sit amongst the trees and sob softly, and who would argue that the creatures she loved did not cease their joyful noises when they heard her?

In one year the sons of Ornon would face the rigors of the third Princes' Trial; but now, at the end of their eighteenth year, there were less hazardous duties to perform. It was at this time that the remainder of the Twenty would be allowed to meet those who would be queen. All had faced terrible dangers in the Torrean Mountains, yet the fearless princes found themselves quaking in terror at this new prospect. All had grilled their mentors mercilessly in the proper things to do, what to say and how to act. The normally stoical mentors found much amusement in the uncertainty of their charges regarding the young women. For the sages, it represented an interlude in the many harsh years of intense training.

Dulok cared little about the prospect of meeting the three girls. His motivation toward the attainment of Survivor did not allow for such trifles. But this was one of the duties required of the Twenty. For this reason, and this alone, would he engage in the ritual.

During the initial few months, the princes would spend two hours out of five days with each of the three girls. These visits would be increased gradually through-out the year, until, shortly before the third Princes' Trial, each son of Ornon would make known to all his choice for queen, should he become Survivor. This decision is binding, and cannot be altered, despite any change of heart or mind on the part of that respective prince in the ensuing years.

It happened by chance that the initial meeting between Dulok and Sallia was the last for both of them. Sallia had found the other eight sons of Ornon to be of an identical mold. All were swaggering, insolent bullies; all were convinced that the title of Survivor would be theirs; all offered grandiose plans for the future of Shadzea under their rule. They were as she thought they would be, and she did not care at all for any. She found the leering Buz to be the most distasteful, and the thought of his oily voice made her shudder. She would offer no encourage-ment to any of them, and she would continue to pray that she would not be selected.

The acid-tongued Dhela had displeased Dulok from the start, and he found the meeting to be interminable. Her beauty had at first stunned him, but it was merely a thin coating for a venomous soul. Ciren had initially captivated him with her warmth, but soon she had begun to voice her unfounded fears and suspicions of everyone she knew. He had tried to talk to her, to help her, but she turned on him, and she would have scratched his face had he not caught her wrist. By the end of the two hours she had calmed again, but the shocked prince found himself relieved that the audience had ended.

No one could blame these two for their apprehension and lack of interest in this final meeting. Sallia awaited

59

the twentieth son in the palace garden, her favorite spot. She felt her garden despoiled by the surly young men who had been here, aimlessly crushing flowers under their heavy sandals. But the garden gave her strength, and she knew that she would require it if the year was to pass.

A door slowly opened, and Dulok entered. Sallia saw him, and she would have averted her eyes, but something about him caused her to stare curiously at the young man. He was clad much like his half brothers, but he resembled few of them. He was tall, quite handsome, with a shock of black hair that was cut squarely just above the shoulders. His demeanor was serious, his face a mask of determination. But there was something in his eyes, something different from those of the others. Even from where she sat she could see the light in them, a soft glow that bespoke suppressed emotions, joy perhaps, or even sorrow. His slow, steady gait was unlike the royal strutting that she had come to loathe. She prayed silently that her judgement was not betraying her.

"I am Dulok, the twentieth son of Ornon, and I bid you well," he recited formally as he paused in front of her.

"I am Sallia, daughter of Bori, and I welcome you," she responded, according to custom.

The two were silent for what seemed like many minutes. Dulok looked away from Sallia, feigning exploration of the garden with his eyes.

"The garden is a beautiful place, is it not, my prince?" Sallia had chosen to break the silence.

"I was just observing that very thing," Dulok replied sheepishly. "I have been here seldom. Would you care to walk through it?"

"You—you are *asking* me?" She appeared nonplussed.

"Of course I'm asking you," said Dulok. "In the name of Doj, what do you mean?"

"You are a prince, and you need only command—"

"*Command?*" Dulok snapped. "I would not *command* you to walk with me. If you want to walk, we'll walk. If you don't, then we'll sit here, or whatever you might want to do."

Dulok was obviously agitated, and he did not appear to be mocking her. Sallia was ashamed that she had opened the matter.

"I—I only meant . . . well, your brothers—"

"My *half* brothers, please!" Dulok grimaced. "Ah! I'm beginning to understand. So you found them to be distasteful bullies, did you?"

"Please, my prince!" she begged. "I didn't mean that!"

"Of course you did," he countered. "Don't worry, for I feel the same."

"You speak the truth, my prince?" she asked.

"Of course! And please, my name is Dulok. You may call me that, *if you wish!*"

"My pr—Dulok?"

"Yes?"

"May I show you about the garden?"

The two grinned at one another, and each knew that this encounter was special. At first they walked in silence; but soon Sallia began to tell Dulok of the things that meant so much to her. Her garden, and all that inhabited it; the soft rain that fell occasionally, bringing life to all that it touched; the poetry of the ancients, epic ballads of romance and courage, of unimagined places and people. Dulok listened, and he smiled as he recalled the similar gentleness of another só long ago. Though he did not express it, he knew that he had discovered something special here, and long forgotten emotions began to well inside him.

The door to the garden opened, and Qual appeared to escort his charge back to the princes' quarters. The two young people looked at each other in astonishment, for hadn't the two hours just begun?

"Dulok, forgive me, for I fear that I chattered at length!" Sallia exclaimed. "You—"

"Do not apologize, Sallia," the prince smiled, "for I enjoyed listening to you. I will look forward to our next meeting."

"And I, my pr—Dulok," she replied shyly.

Sallia watched Dulok as he joined his mentor, nor did she take her eyes from him until he disappeared beyond the garden door. In this serious young prince she saw a different future, and life suddenly took on greater meaning for her. She remained in the garden for hours afterward with the things she loved, and she discovered that the memory of the kindly Dulok made this idyllic place seem far more beautiful.

The year that followed brought great joy to Sallia and Dulok. The other princes stayed away from Sallia, for all had become enamored of the stunning Dhela. Dulok avoided Dhela as if she bore a plague, but he did spend a minimal amount of time with Ciren, for he pitied her, and he wished to help her. He was the only one to show such kindness to the troubled girl, and Sallia admired him for it.

Dulok felt at ease in pouring out his thoughts to the gentle Sallia, for she was receptive to him, and she understood. Emotions dormant for many years in the soul of the youth began to surface, affectivities of tenderness, of caring. His vengeance, until satisfied, would still be the dominant force in his life. But even the throne of Shadzea mattered little to him next to this girl, who, if the gods were with him, might some day be his.

Months after their initial meeting the two found numerous occasions to be together, and neither would doubt that they were much in love. But at first they dared not utter the word, for they knew of the uncertainty regarding their future. They were content merely to be together, to dream together, to share feelings that had long been denied both of them.

Dhela had worked her wiles well on the sons of Ornon, and she was certain that when the time came they would all select her as their queen, all save Dulok. She had especially concentrated on Buz, for she found his ambitions to be as strong as her own, and she believed that he would let nothing stand in his way of the Shadzean throne.

Buz knew of Dulok's relationship with Sallia, and for no other reason but to vex his hated half brother he began spending more time with her, as was his right. Sallia loathed him, and would not speak to him, but this did not deter the first son. To know that it annoyed Dulok made the time well worthwhile. Dhela also chafed at Buz's professed interest in Sallia, but she knew that she would make the perfect queen for Buz, and she did not doubt for a moment that he would choose her.

*   *   *

The year drew quickly to an end, and the time for the third Princes' Trial neared. Each prince had a duty to perform before he undertook this trial, and that was to select the one who would be his queen. The ceremony would be conducted in a large hall within the palace, and all, including Ornon and Otessea, would be present.

Zummek, chief advisor to Ornon and the father of Dhela, presided over the ceremony that day. Dhela, Ciren, and Sallia, similarly clothed in gowns of flowing blue silk, sat on the dais to Ornon's left and faced the gathering. Upon a signal from Zummek a large door was opened, and the sons of Ornon filed in solemnly with their mentors. All stood at attention in deference to the king, who motioned for them to be seated.

"We of Shadzea," began Zummek formerly, "who revere Ornon, our ruler, do gather here in this chamber, under the ever watchful eyes of Doj and Bao, for a great event. Today the Twenty will make known their choice for queen, so that on the day of the Reckoning, at the final moment, there will be no question. As it was done in the time of Boga, the first Survivor, and Dain, the second Survivor, and . . ."

The recitation continued tediously, while the princes squirmed in their seats. The fourteen Survivors were all acknowledged, and a loud roar arose when the name of Ornon was called. The king nodded slightly to the gathering, but his hard expression did not alter.

". . . as has been the custom for centuries," Zummek droned, "the last of the surviving Twenty will make known his choice first. I bid Dulok, the twentieth son, approach the king!"

Dulok stood and walked slowly toward Ornon, but his eyes were not on his hated sire. Instead, he gazed at the girl who sat nearby. She saw him, and she smiled slightly, while the fuming Dhela nudged an elbow into her ribs. Never had Sallia looked as lovely as she did that day, Dulok thought. In this short year alone she had become more of a woman, and his love and respect for her had grown. His reasons for becoming Survivor were now multiplied.

The young prince bowed formally to his father, while Ornon stared impassively at him.

"Dulok, my twentieth son," the ruler intoned. "Have you made your choice of she who would be your queen?"

"I have, Sire," Dulok responded. "I choose Sallia!"

There was little reaction from those assembled, save for the hissing sound that escaped between Dhela's teeth, for all had expected this. Dulok again bowed to the king and returned to Qual, while a scribe noted the selection in a parchment ledger. The next prince was called, and the ritual was repeated.

"Cravik, my eighteenth son," said Ornon. "Have you made your choice of she who would be your queen?"

"I have, Sire," Cravik replied. "I choose Dhela!"

The venomous young woman smiled at her champion, who bowed and returned to his mentor. The ceremony continued, and it went much as expected. Dhela was the choice of all, of Ulus and Xonik, of Esaaz, Korb, and Skoj, of Robbik, the third son. Now only Buz was left, and he approached his father purposely, Ornon nodding his approval of the one that he perceived as most nearly in his image.

"Buz, my first son," said the king. "Have you made your choice of she who would be your queen?"

"I have, Sire," Buz replied. "I choose—Sallia!"

A great murmur arose in the hall at this unexpected revelation. Otessea fumed, while Dhela stamped her foot in indignation. Sallia paled and appeared faint. Dulok leaped to his feet, and he would have confronted Buz had Qual not restrained him. Ornon was also shocked by his son's selection, for he did not understand. Zummek had joined his daughter in an attempt to console her, and the king was forced to restore order to the proceedings.

In the uproar that ensued, no one noticed Ciren rise slowly from her chair and exit the hall through a small servants' door. This poor girl, the choice of no one, was later found on the hard stones outside the palace. She had leaped to her death from an upper balcony.

The hall finally quieted in light of the threats that had been voiced by Ornon. The selection of Buz was duly noted, and the first son returned to his mentor. It happened that Buz and Lonz sat directly behind Dulok and Qual. Dulok, still fuming from Buz's action, tried hard not to show agitation, but Buz knew that the insides of the twentieth son were churning. He leaned over, a smirk on his face, and for the first time in many years words passed between the antagonists.

"You wonder at my choice, do you, *brother?*" Buz mocked. "Then know this: I care nothing for any of them, but I know of your feelings for Sallia. You wish me dead, as I wish you. But until the Survivor is proclaimed, you must live with the knowledge that, should you die, Sallia will belong to me! You will dwell much on this, and who knows? Perhaps the torment of your thoughts will affect your final preparations. Remember well what I have said, Dulok: should I survive, Sallia will be mine!"

Dulok would have grabbed the despicable one by the neck and throttled the life from him, but to do so would

66

mean the loss of everything he had strived for, including the one he loved. He instead turned his attention to the platform, where Zummek was calling the ceremony to a close. He left the hall with the mocking laughter of Buz still ringing in his ears.

Dulok walked in the garden with Sallia on the day preceding his departure for the third Princes' Trial. The choice of Buz was still prevalent in each of their minds, but they did not speak of it at first, for Sallia's concerns were more immediate.

"I will worry much about you while you're away, Dulok, and I will fear for your life," she told him. "What is it that you must do?"

Dulok shook his head. "The nature of the third Princes' Trial is known only to a few, and they are sworn to secrecy. Only when we stand on the threshold do we learn of it."

"But it must be horrible!" she cried. "Oh Dulok, I cannot lose you now. I cannot!"

"Do not fear, my flower," laughed the prince. "No trial is too difficult that it cannot be mastered. I far surpass the others in the skills that have been taught us since childhood. Some of them won't return, but be assured that I will."

"I hope that Buz is among those who do not come back," Sallia stated bitterly.

"You must not speak like this!" Dulok snapped, surprised by the tone of this gentle girl. "To wish death even to one such as him is unlike you."

"I'm sorry my prince, but I mean it. He is a loathsome creature. You must despise him too."

"No more or less than the others," Dulok lied. He had

67

never told Sallia of Buz's part in the death of Daynea, nor even of his mother's demise, for he did not wish to share his hatred, lest his uncharacteristic desire for cruel vengeance be accidently revealed.

"But he appears to hate you above the rest. Why is this?"

"As a child he would bully the others, and it was left up to me to put him in his place. He has never forgotten, nor could he ever forgive. He will carry this bitterness to the grave with him some day, of that you can be certain."

"Come, enough talk of him," Sallia chided. "Tomorrow you will be gone, and I will not see you again for—for many days. Let's enjoy the rest of the afternoon."

"You are right," Dulok laughed. "Today is for the two of us."

And the day sped by, as most of theirs always seemed to. Qual arrived conveniently late to gather his charge, and Dulok was grateful to the wily mentor for his consideration. For the last time before the third Princes' Trial the two faced one another, their hands clasped.

"You might never return to me, Dulok," said Sallia, her expression grave. "Please, do not contradict, for you know yourself that it is a possibility. You have given me the most wonderful year of my life, and there is something I desire you to know: I love you, my prince, and I would not choose to live without you."

"I love you too, my flower," said Dulok, and he smiled as he crushed Sallia to him. "I have from the first. You can be certain that the knowledge of your love will sustain me through whatever I must face. I *will* return to you."

Their lips met, albeit fleetingly, for the passions that swelled suddenly within the pair could scarce be satisfied at that moment. The quivering Dulok then joined his fidgety mentor, and with a final glance at the tear-streaked girl he exited the garden. Sallia remained there until darkness fell, and she prayed to the Shadzean deities that her lover would be returned safely to her.

CHAPTER FIVE

THE CITY OF MADNESS

Nine princes of Shadzea, the remainder of the Twenty, departed the City of Kings early the next morning. They traveled toward the northwest, their ultimate destination a well-kept secret. Even the head of the Shadzean guard that accompanied them did not know where they were bound, but the mentors made sure that the party never strayed from the correct path. A number of the princes speculated that they were on their way to the Telliun Ocean, there perhaps to do battle with some unimaginable monster from the depths of the sea, or even to clash head-on with the piratical villains who made the City of Rogues their stronghold. Dulok, alone from the others, chose not to ponder on the nature of the trial, for he knew that all must eventually face it, regardless of what it entailed.

Some of the road was well beaten, though in most places there was no path to speak of, and they were slowed considerably. Still, on the fourth day after departure the walls of a city were sighted, and even the most fearless of the Twenty blanched as they realized that this was their destination.

The City of Madness represented one of the most unspeakable places in all of Shadzea. Here, within its ragged walls, were put the dregs of the kingdom, the criminally insane, the depraved, the perpetrators of the most debased atrocities and perversions. In this mockery of a city they would live out their foul existence, though the life expectancy was not lengthy. One never knew whether he broke bread with a man who dismembered young girls for the pure ecstasy of it, or whether he bedded a woman who had carved to death her entire family. These demented souls ran free, for no overseer would share the confines of the city with their like. Heavily armed guards surrounded the city, and it was their responsibility to see that all remained within, as well as to see that they were provided with food and water. These outposts were well back from the walls, for the stench that emanated from the City of Madness could only have been duplicated by the wretched effluvium that poured forth from the dankest, most foul pits of Esh.

After advising the local guard of their presence, the party continued to the gates of the city. But before they neared the walls the stench overwhelmed many of them, and they retched noisily on the dusty ground. Among this group was Esaaz and Robbik, as well as the mentor of Korb. Dulok was appalled by the vile smell, but he fought within himself to retain his composure. He saw that Buz was conducting a similar battle, and that at times he appeared to be losing.

Eventually, all reached the gates, and in time the stench did not bother them nearly as much. Lonz sat high atop his horse, while the princes and their mentors dismounted, and for the third time in their lives they

71

stood on the threshold of another trial—on the brink of death.

"Princes of Shadzea, hear and obey!" Lonz shouted. "You of the Twenty that have survived the first nineteen years of your lives have come to the gates of the City of Madness, and here, beginning this day, you will endure the third of the Princes' Trials. You will enter the gates of this city one by one, and you will disperse within, so that chance encounters will be minimal. The gates will be closed behind you. In seven days, when the sun is high, the gates will reopen, and you will emerge whole, or not at all. The ranks of the Twenty have always been greatly reduced during this trial in the past. In your minds you will convince yourselves that you will not be among that number. Survival is Life; Life is Survival!"

The princes looked upon each other in astonishment. What horrors within these walls could compare with the manifold dangers they had encountered upon the Torrean Mountains? Fear of the unknown is perhaps the worst fear that man could possess. That their only goal was to emerge alive manifested these fears, for they had learned from the earliest that survival was their prime motivation. To survive amidst the unknown was by far the greatest challenge yet in their young, rigid lives.

It took four guards to disengage the enormous bolt that kept the City of Madness a prison. The princes stood in single file, nervously awaiting their entry. The heavy portal was cracked open just enough to allow one body ingress. This initial body belonged to Buz, whose entry necessitated the assistance of his mentor and a guard. The door was then pulled shut, and it was minutes later before Robbik made his entry. And so it went, until only Dulok stood without, awaiting his turn. The portal swung open, and the twentieth son stepped forward, to what only Bao could know.

The door slammed shut behind him, and he could hear the scraping noise as the huge bolt was reset in its place. His first impression was the renewed awareness of the stench. It did not seem possible, but within the walls it was infinitely worse than it had been outside. From where he stood he bore witness to a maze of narrow, dusty streets that disappeared into the heart of the city amidst assorted, haphazard twists and turns. Surely the city's road work had been designed by some past inhabitant. The most appalling feature of these streets was the uncounted piles of refuse and excrement that littered them. It appeared that the streets were never cleaned; at best, the filth was shoved into even greater heaps along the side of the road when it became too much of a barrier. The horrified prince could now understand the reason for the foul stench of this place.

The three men were only yards from him when he first became aware of their presence, so intent was he on examining his surroundings. He wheeled quickly, his hand instinctively reaching for his sword; but he was unarmed, for no weapons were allowed here. The men shuffled slowly toward him, and they did not appear to be hostile. They were small in comparison to the strapping Dulok, and what little clothes they wore were ragged and filthy. The apparent leader was a heavy fellow, much more so than the others. He displayed an evil countenance, and he grinned through a mouthful of yellow, broken teeth. The faces of the other two were dull, expressionless. The leader motioned for them to halt, and he alone approached Dulok.

"New citizen?" he rasped.

"What?" asked Dulok.

"New citizen?" he repeated. "You are a new citizen?" Dulok nodded vaguely. "Then you must be taken to Egowol! Come! You must be taken to Egowol!"

He looked toward his cronies, as if for approval. The dullards nodded their heads and gibbered excitedly. Dulok, not seeking trouble, was determined to play their game.

"And where shall I find this—Egowol?" he asked.

The leader pointed at one of the winding streets. "All must know where to find Egowol," he said in his grating voice. The others continued to nod vigorously. "Come! Come! I will show you. Hurry!"

The leader shambled up the twisting travesty of a street, and with each shuffling step he motioned for Dulok to follow. Dulok quietly complied, though he was careful to sidestep the heaps of filth that virtually paved the road. The two chattering idiots brought up the rear, and neither they nor their leader exhibited any interest in avoiding the refuse beneath their feet. Such signs of depravity caused the normally staid Dulok to shudder.

The twentieth son of Ornon, possible heir to the throne of Shadzea, now followed his demented host along the senseless, zigzagging streets of the City of Madness. They passed others along the way; men, women, and— the gods help them—children! To be born of parents in such a place was beyond imagination. Surely no child could be brought here from the outside purposely!

After many minutes of seemingly aimless wandering, the leader appeared to lose track of the task he had originally set out to do. At times he would stop and scratch his head, resuming the trek only after staring at Dulok for a moment. Once he discovered a small loaf of hard, moldy bread on the ground. He sat down amidst the excrement and began to gnaw on it, and soon his fellows had joined him.

Dulok stood disgustedly and watched the trio hiss and sputter at each other as they tried to divide the putrid tidbit. But soon his patience wore thin, and he decided to leave them to their repast. He doubted that they would even notice he was gone, or remember that he had been there. He walked away slowly, and upon reaching the intersection of another street he hastened his steps. But no sooner did he turn the corner than he knew that his departure had been noticed.

"A new citizen runs free!" The raspy voice echoed through the narrow alleys. "A new citizen runs free! He has not seen Egowol! Quick, find him, stop him!"

Dulok began to run blindly through the alleys. He passed others as he ran, and he was alert to any interference, but none expressed the least interest in him. Without prior knowledge of these confusing streets he found himself entering one cul-de-sac after another, and each time he was forced to retrace his steps until a more accessible lane could be found. He lost all sense of direction, and after many desperate minutes of flight he found himself back where he had started. His hosts awaited him with glee.

"Ah, here is our new citizen!" grinned the leader. "So he didn't leave us after all. Come citizen, and we will—"

His sentence went unfinished, for Dulok was of no mind to see Egowol, whatever that was. He turned and fled, and this time the three took up the pursuit, screaming and gibbering as they tried to narrow the distance between them and their erstwhile guest. They were no match against the speed of the swift Dulok, but they knew this maze well, and he did not. Once again the prince found himself in a cul-de-sac, and the walls that surrounded him offered no footholds. At the entrance to the blind alley stood the trio.

"You sought to escape us, new citizen!" the leader shrieked, his eyes now ablaze with the fires of madness. "Egowol will be displeased. There is no escape for you now. You will come with us!"

The leader moved toward him slowly, the two chattering dullards at his heels. Dulok knew that they would be no match against him, but he regretted having to injure them, for he had wished to avoid trouble while he was there. He shrugged his shoulders and went forth to meet them, for he knew that there was no choice.

A fourth figure suddenly appeared at the entrance behind the trio, and Dulok halted in his tracks as he gazed disbelievingly at the new arrival. The fellow was a black, probably from one of the distant island nations, and the first that Dulok had ever seen. He stood a full head taller than seven feet, and his glistening arms and legs bulged with huge knots of muscles that told of incredible, limitless strength. But above all this, the most noticeable feature was the fellow's head, which made it a travesty to call him human. The head was twice the size of any normal pate, with not a hair on any part of it. Instead, it was covered with masses of wrinkled, fleshy tumors, these so numerous that they all but hid the ears and the O-shaped mouth. The nostrils were but tiny pinpricks in the middle of the hideous face, while two bloodshot eyes stared menacingly from deep, cavelike sockets. Dulok could not, in his worst nightmares, imagine the atrocities that one such as this could have perpetrated to land him here. It would have taken a Shadzean regiment to subdue him.

Dulok knew that the only way free of this trap would be by the use of his wits. Without hesitation he raced toward the group, and he saw that this tactic surprised them. In a single motion he bowled the leader over and struck the others with his fists. The trio fell to the ground, stunned. Now only the immense black stood between himself and escape. The fellow's bulk covered much of the alley, but Dulok was sure that along with this size went sluggishness. He tried to dodge the black and run past him, but the fellow's surprising speed was on par with his strength. Dulok could find no egress, and slowly he was being forced back into the cul-de-sac.

As intent as he was on this fearsome adversary, Dulok forgot about the others. But they had quickly recovered, and now they swarmed all over his back. He fought them off as best he could, but during the brief engagement the black was able to grab him and pin his arms behind his back. He tried to free himself, but he was as a babe against the steellike strength in this grotesque fellow's sinews. His struggles only caused him greater pain, so he ceased. It did not appear as if the black wished to cause him deliberate injury.

"Come, new citizen," rasped the leader cheerily, as if nothing had happened. "Come, for now you *shall* see Egowol."

The trio led the way through the maze of alleys, while the subdued Dulok, his arms pinioned tightly by the giant, followed. The narrow streets opened suddenly into a vast plaza, probably the center of this accursed city. A shiny edifice occupied the heart of the square, and Dulok was amazed at the sight. This building, unlike the mud and brick structures he had seen throughout the city, was built of marble, and its beautiful lines would not have been out of place in the City of Kings. Surely this was a relic of some long dead civilization, for no mind that currently occupied this ghastly place could have conceived of such splendor.

"Behold, the Temple of Egowol!" announced the leader. "Come, new citizen, and you shall see Egowol. Yes, you shall indeed see Egowol!"

The rest of the group, all save the silent black, chortled uncontrollably at his words, but Dulok felt certain that there was nothing humorous here. He forced himself to look up into the hideous face of his captor, as if for some assurance, but he could read nothing in the deep-set eyes. He could only wait and see what they had planned for him.

Twelve broad steps, each perfectly placed between tall, ornamented columns, led upward to a heavy door carved of obsidian. The trio grunted as they tried to push it open, but they could not. The black, holding Dulok's two hands in one of his, shoved the portal open with little effort. They then strode through a long, dark hallway, where well-worn tapestries, surely once beautiful, lined the walls. Into a circular chamber the prince of Shadzea was led, and in the center of this vast room Dulok could see a great commotion, for numerous people milled about and chattered loudly. As they sensed the presence of the new arrivals the group parted, and in the dim light Dulok was able to perceive the core of their interest.

Before the prince was a raised platform some fifteen feet square, but no more than two feet high. The throne of Ornon sat atop a similar dais in the great place of his home city, but no such chair ornamented the one in the Temple of Egowol. There was something on this platform, however, and Dulok strained to identify it. As his vision became more accustomed to the dim light he saw that the shape atop the dais was alive, and that it undulated slowly, almost rhythmically. It raised itself up on one arm, and Dulok saw that it was—a man! He was no bigger than a child, but he was indeed a man, a horribly old, grotesquely wrinkled human being. The taut, leathery skin gave his face the appearance of a death's-head, while his ribs could be counted clearly, even from a distance. A few thin, gray wisps of hair still clung atop the skull. He might have been a hundred years old, and then again he might have borne witness to the proclamation of the first Survivor. It was impossible to tell.

The withered figure feebly raised a gnarled hand in the air and issued a weak signal with one bent finger. Instantly the people who surrounded the dais became excited, as did Dulok's captors, all save the black. The leader, through his dementia, leered at Dulok and shrieked:

"Egowol dines! Egowol dines! How fortunate you are, new citizen, how fortunate we all are, for Egowol dines!"

Two men appeared, carrying a naked, unattractive woman. This woman, whether cognizant of her fate or not, displayed no fear, but instead writhed and moaned in ecstasy. She was deposited on the dais in front of Egowol, and while she continued to squirm a third madman rushed forth from the group and thrust a long, narrow dagger deep into her heart. The blade was then removed, and a thin jet of blood spurted high in the air. But before too much had been wasted, the first two men lifted Egowol and deposited him on top of the dead girl. He was positioned so that his thick, flabby lips were suctioned to the area surrounding the puncture made by the piercing steel. In this way the escaping blood squirted into the toothless mouth, and amidst much gurgling and sucking, the ghoul feasted.

All had happened with such blinding speed that the alert Dulok was at first unable to grasp the horror of it. But now, as those around him groaned ecstatically at the repast of the creature on the dais, he found himself overwhelmed by the sight. He would have run to the dais and torn the fiend to shreds with his hands, but he remembered his captor. The black was also beginning to succumb to the blood ritual, and his taut grip on Dulok had lessened slightly. The young prince, calling on his own strength, as well as the strength of desperation and terror, lifted the weighty black high above his head and hurled him toward the platform, where he fell with a sickening crunch atop the ancient ghoul, the dead woman, and one of the men. The gore of the crushed victims spattered those closest to the dais, and this set off a new wave of delirium amongst the acolytes of Egowol. They fell upon the platform and began to rend anything they could lay their hands on. Even the stunned black fell under the sheer weight of numbers, and the first and last sound that Dulok heard him utter was a loud, blood-freezing shriek that resounded through the chamber and momentarily stilled all who heard it.

The horrified Dulok, not wishing to remain in this temple of death any longer, bowled over two of the closest fiends in his haste to exit. He left the way he had been brought in, and even the heavy door offered no resistance to his mad flight. Down the steps and into the plaza he ran, his eyes ablaze with the atrocities they had witnessed. Those who saw him cared little, for did not one such as he belong here with them? He did not know in which direction he fled, but only after it became physically impossible for him to continue did he stop. He fell to the ground and panted heavily, his head buried in his hands.

Little more than a minute passed before he sensed the dull thud of footfalls in the alley that he occupied, but only when they stopped nearby did he dare look up. A large fellow stood over him, and he appeared to be another dullard. But a hint of recognition pierced Dulok's confused brain, and he realized that it was Ulus, the sixteenth son of Ornon. Ulus might have destroyed him where he sat, for he could offer no resistance, but he merely stood as one paralyzed. Finally he spoke in a voice that left little doubt as to his terror:

"If one must live through this place to become the Survivor, then surely I am not of the mettle for the task, my brother. I have seen too much in only hours, yet I am expected to stay for days. Nay, Dulok, I leave this place to you and the others."

Ulus raised his hands to his head almost ceremoniously, and with the strength of madness he gave a mighty twist. His neck broken, he fell to the hard earth next to Dulok. For the first time in his life Dulok felt sadness at the death of one of his half brothers.

The encounter with Ulus served to bring the distraught young man to his senses. His purpose in being here again surfaced, and survival became uppermost in his mind. He would ignore the horrors that surrounded him in the City of Madness, and in seven days he would emerge, whole in body, whole in mind. He would seek out a place of concealment for the duration, there perhaps to block out the realities of the demented beings that carried

81

on their mindless existence within the walls of this metropolis of death.

For hours Dulok wandered through the narrow streets, not really knowing what he sought. Soon, even amidst the pollution of refuse and dung, he realized that he suffered the pangs of hunger, the tortures of thirst. He knew now that his will to survive was still intact, for to see what he had seen, to live what he had lived, might have negated such needs in others. But how would he acquire what was necessary, since he had been given no coins before entering the city? He knew what the answer would be, and the thought did not trouble him as greatly as he imagined it might. He, the twentieth son of Ornon, a prince of Shadzea, would become a common thief!

But of what use, as he was to realize later, would coins be in such a place? Food and drink were everywhere for the taking, provided you were fortunate enough to acquire it before it became contaminated. The inns and marketplaces were barely tended, and Dulok took whatever he desired. He made certain to leave that which was perishable, and he especially decided to forgo meat. He gathered enough for at least three days, and he continued his search for a place of concealment.

The sicknesses of the mind ran rampant through the streets as Dulok continued his search, but he exerted great power of will in an effort to block them out. He saw a woman fall from the roof of a building into the street below, and as she writhed and whimpered in the filth, her bones shattered, unseeing strollers walked over her broken body as if she were no more than the excrement beneath their feet. She died, quite mercifully, before he could render aid. He saw a man hanging from a tall post, a thick rope around his neck, his skin bloated and pasty from the many days he had been there. Two children held onto either of his legs, swinging in youthful, innocent glee.

Once Dulok entered a tiny hut that he thought empty, only to find two women crouched in opposite corners, apparently terrified. He tried to talk to them, but they came at him like crazed cats, and they would have scratched his eyes out had he not fought them off. He exited the hut quickly, uninjured but shaken, and as his search dragged on he became more intent. Because of this he did not notice the pair of eyes upon him, eyes that had watched him from the time he had left the Temple of Egowol.

Soon Dulok turned a sharp corner, nearly bumping into an elderly man as he did. The man showed no physical defects, and his wizened face bore a pair of intelligent-looking eyes that appeared to brighten as he espied Dulok.

"Ah, a newcomer," he stated gleefully. "Are you perhaps a prince of Shadzea, here for one of your trials?" He offered Dulok his hand in friendship.

"But how could you know of this?" asked the surprised Dulok, taking the hand. "Who are you?"

The man's expression changed suddenly, and he began to jabber: "Why, I am Boga, the first Survivor; and Kerno, the fourth Survivor; and, of course, Sothor, from the forest. Do you not recognize me? *Haahaa!*"

He grinned broadly, and Dulok saw that his teeth were filed to sharpened points. Before he could react the old man had sunk his teeth into his hand, and already he had drawn blood. Dulok yelped in pain, and he thrust the crazed soul from him. The old man smashed against a wall and crumpled to the ground in a heap, a delirious smile still upon his face. The sickened prince fled in horror, and the eyes that watched him felt tears well, for they pitied the helpless young man.

Darkness had nearly fallen when Dulok finally found what he sought, and he was thankful, for the prospect of wandering the foul city at night appalled him. He had entered a small building, once apparently a shop, but now empty. A crudely built ladder led to a tiny attic. He climbed the ladder cautiously, fearful of what he might discover in the rafters, but to his relief it was empty. He pulled the ladder up after him, now certain that he would be safe.

The pair of eyes stood outside the shop, and they watched the ladder disappear above. They now knew where he was, that he was most likely to remain there. They departed quickly, for darkness was an enemy to all here.

Dulok had been in the attic for four full days, venturing out only once to acquire more food and water. Through cracks in the attic wall he could see and hear the perpetration of more cruel, sadistic, insane acts, but he ignored them, for in his time here his mind had grown numb. To survive, to leave here, to see Sallia once again. Yes, Sallia! The thought of her beauty and gentleness would sustain him, as he had told her it would. She was all that mattered. She, and—vengeance! But the thought of his revenge paled by comparison to the horrors in the City of Madness. Never could he perform such atrocities—or could he, since the proposed victims were the cowardly assassins of his mother? Only time, and the will of the gods, would reveal the truth.

On the fifth day there he heard a noise below, and he

became silent. Twice before others had occupied the lower floor, but for no more than an hour or two. Now he waited, and he hoped that whoever was there would soon leave.

"Dulok! Dulok, please!" The hushed voice came from below. The prince stiffened, but he did not answer.

"Dulok, I know you are up there. Slide the wood and look down!" The voice was pleading with him.

Dulok shoved the board away from the hole and peered down cautiously. In the middle of the room, looking up at him, stood a young girl. She appeared sane, but Dulok knew that such an appearance in this place was deceiving.

"Who are you?" he snapped. "How do you know my name, and my place of hiding?"

"My name is Lecca, and I am a friend of one who would talk to you. She has known for days where you hide."

"Who is she, and what does she want of me?" asked Dulok suspiciously. "Why does she not come herself?"

"She is at times incoherent, and she fears that you would disbelieve her. I wish to assure you that she is sincere, and her greatest wish is to see you safely from this place. What she has to tell you will do you no good here."

"Bring her to me," ordered Dulok, still wary. "But bring no one else, and be sure none see you enter or leave."

"Thank you, Sire," said the girl, and she hurried off.

Dulok brooded during her absence, for he could not imagine who in this city, save his half brothers, knew of him. Through the cracks he watched the street carefully, but it was nearly an hour before the girl returned. There was another with her. The two cautiously entered the empty shop, and Dulok peered down from the attic, but he could not see the stranger's face. She had long hair, and she did not look up.

"Quickly, Dulok, lower the ladder," the girl instructed.

"Only the woman comes up," the prince demanded.

"Agreed," Lecca replied. "I will return for her in two hours. Do not be frightened by her lapses, but listen well to her words."

The woman slowly climbed the ladder, and when she stood on the floor of the attic Dulok pulled the ladder up and covered the hole. He turned his attention to the woman, but in the dim light he was unable to see her clearly. She approached him slowly, the haggard, troubled face stirring no traces of recognition in his brain. There was no doubt that this woman was mad, and yet in her eyes he sensed a coherent urgency, a pleading on her part for him to grasp the last traces of sanity that she possessed, however deep within her tormented soul they might be. Her eyes met his, and she studied his face intently.

"Yes, you are surely Dulok, the twentieth son of Ornon," she wheezed. "Listen to me carefully, Dulok, for I've something to tell you."

On the seventh day, at the noon hour, the gates to the City of Madness were again opened, and five young men emerged. They were Korb, and Buz, and Esaaz, and Xonik, and Dulok. Xonik had made it to the gate with his last thread of sanity, but once outside the tenuous strand snapped, and before he could be restrained he had throttled the life from his mentor. The gates were reopened, and Xonik was returned to the city for all time.

The trial was formally pronounced at an end by Lonz,

and the names of Robbik, Skoj, Xonik, Ulus, and Cravik were recited for the last time. The subdued party then made their way back to the City of Kings, to home. The mentors sensed the anguish that their charges had suffered, and they did not trouble them with inane conversation. All had emerged from this trial as different men, but none more so than Dulok.

CHAPTER SIX

THE THEFT OF THE STONE

The four remaining princes of Shadzea had long since quitted their shared quarters by the end of the twentieth year, for a new phase of their preparations had begun. Every third day each prince spent one hour with Ornon, where they learned the intricacies of ruling a kingdom, things which their years of rigid training could not possibly have taught them. Most would eventually find this facet of their lives to be most difficult, for Ornon was a surly individual, and he considered much of the time spent with his sons to be wasted effort. After all, he reasoned, only one would succeed him to the throne. He had even thought of altering the Rite of the Twenty for the first time in hundreds of years, but his council advised him against this.

Though none could say for sure, it was generally believed that Ornon's time with Buz offered him the most gratification. No one understood why, even from the earliest, this son had been of special interest to the king. Such a weakness, even one so minute, was unbefitting a Shadzean ruler. Still, all knew that the reigning Survivor had little to say in the matter regarding his successor. The throne of Shadzea could only be won by the initiative of the individual.

A small, shadowy figure strode the nearly deserted corridors in the dark hours. He found the particular door he sought, and after assuring himself that no one was within earshot he rapped softly four times.

"Who knocks?" challenged the voice from within.

"It is I," replied the figure. "Ornon told me to come."

The door opened quickly, and the figure glided through.

"He is ready?" asked the visitor.

"Most ready, and quite willing," answered the other.

"Good. I do not wish to waste time. The lessons shall begin."

In the time that he spent with Ornon, Dulok grew to loathe him even more. He fought within himself so as not to betray his emotions, for many were the times that he wished to end the king's life prematurely. But this would not do, and he knew it. He spent his allotted time with Ornon, and he learned his lessons well. Never did he allow his foul-tempered parent to see him as anything more than a worthy possibility for the throne of Shadzea.

The love between Dulok and Sallia continued to grow. By the time she was twenty, a year younger than Dulok, she had blossomed to full womanhood. Her simple looks of years past had matured into great natural beauty, and she became the envy of all who chanced to set eyes upon her. Even Esaaz and Korb now regretted their choice of Dhela, for her appearance had diminished in their eyes under the bite of her acid tongue.

Buz continued to spend his allotted time with Sallia, his motive still to bait Dulok. But as Sallia changed, so did Buz. Soon his selfish motive gave way to a new desire, and the urge to possess her became great. He started to treat her differently, more graciously. She did not understand the change, nor did she care, for her heart belonged only to Dulok. But she was relieved to find that in the time she was forced to spend with Buz, she did not have to be subjected to his swaggering, boastful ways.

The twenty-second birthday of the princes was at hand, and each gave serious thought to the selection of the fourth and final Princes' Trial, one that would be worthy in the eyes of Ornon. Korb made the first selection, a choice heartily approved by the king. In the Telliun Ocean there dwelt a strange and terrible beast, the zkreel. This monster preyed on the helpless fishing fleets, and few had ever lived to tell about it. Korb would depart from the City of Fishers in a small craft. He would seek out the zkreel, and he would destroy it, or be destroyed by it. Should he prevail, he would place the head of the leviathan at the feet of Ornon.

Esaaz, not to be outdone by this, selected a trial that made all present gasp. He would duplicate the Trial of Death once chosen by Kerno. He would travel north, deep into the Forest of Sothor, and in the distant hills he would slay the legendary azkor, the immense, white-furred beast that dwelt there. Ornon had no choice but to approve this trial, for even he himself would not have made it. The name of Esaaz suddenly rose to the front on the tongues of all, and it was generally conceded that one who could endure such a trial would surely be a worthy Survivor.

Esaaz and Korb had long since departed, but as yet

Dulok and Buz had not yet chosen their respective trials. Dulok longed for one even more worthy than the others, while Buz, whose valor had diminished with each succeeding trial, was merely biding his time. None save Lonz knew that, upon entering the City of Madness for the third trial, Buz had been whisked away by one within who had expected him, and had spent the seven days in safety and comfort.

A message arrived for Ornon one day from the City of Gods, and the words portended disaster for Shadzea on a monumental scale. At first Ornon did not dare to believe what he was reading, but the messenger grimly acknowledged its truth: the Stone of Bao had been stolen! The jewel that represented the very life of the kingdom, if one could believe the legends, had been taken from the Great Hall of Bao, the red priests that guarded it having been murdered. Only one priest was still alive when the blasphemy was discovered, and with his final breath he had uttered a single word: *Fashaar!*

Dulok requested an audience with Ornon that same day, and was begrudgingly granted it. Turmoil prevailed in Ornon's throne room as Dulok and his mentor approached. Ornon scowled as he saw them.

"You choose a strange time to see me, Dulok," the king growled. "This will be most important, I presume. You are aware of what has happened?"

"I am, Sire," Dulok replied as he bowed stiffly. "It is the reason why I have come. To march an army into the Desert of Craters would mean death for many, for you cannot fight the Fashaars on their own ground. One man alone might fare better. I propose, as my fourth Princes' Trial, to retrieve the Stone of Bao and return it to its rightful place in the City of Gods!"

Ornon stared thoughtfully at his twentieth son, the barest hint of respect showing in his eyes.

"Your point is well taken," the king stated. "But without the protection of the stone, all Shadzea will surely perish. What matter then if I waste an army?"

"What assurance do we have that this is so, other than the legends?" Dulok asked. "The Forest of Sothor has been silent for these hundreds of years, and little of the black arts have been carried on in the kingdom. Would it not be best to confine the knowledge of the stone's disappearance to the two cities for the time being, and allow me to seek it out?"

Ornon quickly called together his council, and the plan of Dulok was made known to them. After much discussion, their decision was conveyed to Dulok and Qual.

"As King of Shadzea I approve of your plan," announced Ornon. "You will be allowed a period of one year, as you would with any Trial of Death you might have selected. At the end of this year you will be mourned as dead, and I will proceed accordingly. So let the choice of Dulok be entered in the book!"

Dulok and Qual offered their respect to Ornon with a nod of the head, and they turned to depart. Buz and Lonz chose this moment to enter the throne room, for a similar thought had occurred to them. But when they saw Dulok and his mentor, and overheard Ornon's orders to cease preparations, they knew that they were too late. Buz glared hatefully at his half brother, but Dulok chose not to taunt him, for this was not his way.

"You have chosen a worthy trial, *brother!*" Buz spat. "Poor Sallia. She will not see you after today, for you will not return. I will get to know her better before I select my

92

own trial, since you will not be around to monopolize her time. Yes, I believe I shall enjoy this!"

Qual pulled his charge away, lest his temper overcome him. But Dulok had come too far to let such an incident grate at him. The thought of Buz and Sallia together made him shudder, and he knew that he must see her before he left the city. He advised Qual of this, and the mentor approved.

Their appointed time had come and gone, but still Sallia awaited Dulok in the garden. He had never been late before, but she knew that something was afoot in the palace, and that Dulok must, in some way, be involved. Still, she was concerned. But when the door to the garden opened, and Dulok entered, all her apprehensions were quickly forgotten, and she flew into his arms.

"I worried for you, Dulok," she scolded gently after they had disengaged. "Could you not advise me that you would be detained?"

"Much has happened today, my flower, and my mind has been otherwise occupied. The Stone of Bao has been taken from the temple in the City of Gods. I leave tomorrow to find and return it, for Ornon has sanctioned this as my final Princes' Trial."

"Oh, Dulok!" she cried. "Never have I dreaded the arrival of a day as I have this one. Though I know what you must do, still I curse the accidents of our birth that prevent us from sharing a simple life together. Once again I fear that you will not return to me."

"And once again I tell you that I *will* be back," stated Dulok strongly. "There is more at stake for me now than ever before. Nothing can prevent my return. You have my word on that!"

Sallia heard him, and she believed him, for she knew

that they would always be together, whether in this world or another. She did not express this to Dulok, for she knew that such talk troubled him. Instead they spent the day in each other's arms, and for the first time, to their unbounded joy, they satisfied their heretofore restrained passions, this in defiance of the Shadzean laws. The discreet Qual did not appear at the appointed hour to collect his charge, and only after the sun had fallen did the radiant Sallia chase her lover away, for she knew that he would require sleep for the long quest that began the next morning. They parted with much hesitation, and Sallia prayed softly for a quick, successful end to Dulok's Trial of Death.

The prince departed the City of Kings early the next morning. He sat atop a fine black stallion, his favored steed. He had trained this horse from the time it was a colt. None were at the gates of the city to see him off, which was as he preferred. But Qual and Sallia, those who cared for him most, stood at the window of one of the lofty palace towers and sadly watched his departure, until only a puff of dust could be seen near the horizon.

There were others in the palace that morning who watched Dulok depart, but none shared in the melancholy of the two who loved him. There was the leering Buz, and Lonz, his ambitious mentor; there was Dhela, and Zummek her father; even the sire of the twentieth son watched his departure from the solitude of his chamber, and he felt relieved, as if imminent danger had been temporarily wrested from his midst. He could not understand this feeling.

Dulok pushed the fine steed to its limits, and despite the rugged terrain he arrived at the gates of the City of Gods near sunset of the third day. He was well received as a prince of Shadzea, even though the city was in a turmoil over the loss of its prize. He spent only one day there, absorbing all he could regarding the theft. How the Fashaars even entered the city was a mystery to all, for their leathery skin and hawklike noses easily distinguished them from the men of Shadzea. It was believed that they received help from within, but the slit throats of the priests in the Great Hall of Bao silenced their tongues, and it was questionable whether this theory would ever be proven.

The harried priests swore to Dulok that Sothor, the black magician, still lived, and that in the great forest to the north he continued to instruct willing acolytes in the forbidden rites of Esh, in the belief that one day the minions of the underworld would crawl up from their pits of slime and lay claim to all the known world. Sothor would surely know of the theft of the stone, but just its disappearance would not be sufficient, for in order to call forth the Dark Ones he must first be certain of the stone's destruction. The Fashaars would doubtless not destroy the stone, for they were known to be a greedy race, and to those who stole it the jewel would be worth much.

"But where would they take such a treasure?" Dulok had asked the head priest. "The Desert of Craters is said to be endless. Where would one even begin to look?"

"That is for only the gods to know," the priest had answered. "So far they have offered no assistance, for the loss of the stone must have greatly disturbed them. I fear, my prince, that you are on your own."

Aware that he might lose much time before the gods proffered their aid, Dulok left the City of Gods and drove his stallion eastward. For the first time he realized the magnitude of the hopeless task he had chosen as his fourth trial. Better to do battle with a zkreel or an azkor. Perhaps the destruction of Blotono, chieftain of the City of Rogues, would have been a better choice. All of these tasks had a visible end to them, one way or another. But this? Surely this was folly! He could scour the desert for years, provided the sun did not first bleach his bones, and not even find one Fashaar, much less those he sought.

It was a troubled young prince of Shadzea who neared the Kobur River late one afternoon, days after departing the City of Gods.

CHAPTER SEVEN

THE OASIS OF GHADI

The dry desert wind stirred up small eddies of sand in front of the horse and rider, but they advanced undeterred, for this was their element, their home. But this same malignant breeze whistled in the ears of the rider, and he could hear no sounds; nor could the sensitive nostrils of his hardy pony detect any unfamiliar scent, for the one who stalked them was downwind, this by design.

The stalker waited impatiently, his well-trained steed tethered silently behind the huge dune. He watched as the robed son of the desert drew nearer, still nearer, but not until the last moment, when the rider was directly below him, did he pounce atop him. Both horse and rider crumpled to the sand from the force of the blow. The frenzied horse whinnied loudly and regained its feet quickly, but it did not stray far. The rider, a heavy man, felt his right arm twisted tightly behind his back, and he submitted meekly to his assailant, for the blow had winded him.

"Offer no resistance, Fashaar, or you will pay dearly

for it," the strong voice ordered.

"You need but command, and Gomol obeys!" the Fashaar whined.

"You are a thief, Gomol," the other stated.

"But *fenda*, I have stolen nothing!" Gomol protested. "I am not—*aayiiee!*"

His arm was twisted even tighter, and the sharp edge of a knife found its way to his throat.

"You are a thief, and you have stolen something of great value," the attacker continued. "But what you have stolen is worthless to you unless you can find someone to purchase it. Where would you take such an item?"

"But fenda, I swear to you!" Gomol pleaded. "An honest man such as myself knows not the ways of criminals. I—*pleeease!*"

The blade barely nicked his skin, but he could feel the droplets of blood that trickled down his neck, mingled with beads of sweat.

"The item is of enormous value, and as such it would require one of vast wealth to purchase it," the fellow continued, deaf to the words of Gomol. "Who, in the Desert of Craters, has such wealth?"

Gomol, certain that his next lie would be his last, blurted out the answer that his deadly attacker had been waiting for. "Ibdan! I would take it to Ibdan, the great seikh of the northern desert!" he sputtered. "He is said to be the wealthiest man in all the lands, and he yearns to possess items of great value. Why, some even say—"

"Silence!" ordered the other, removing the blade from Gomol's throat. "You will guide me there, for I wish to find this Ibdan."

"Fenda, please, it is a great distance from here," Gomol groaned. "I must return to my own tents, for my women—*aayiiee!*"

His arm was twisted so tightly that he was certain it would break. The tip of the knife was pushed against his back, and Gomol's spine almost snapped from the tension.

"I would as soon leave your fat bones in the sand for the vultures to pick clean," the man snapped. "I toy with you no further. Will you lead me to the tents of Ibdan?"

"On second thought, fenda, I just remembered that I have reasons for traveling north myself," hissed Gomol through gritted teeth. "It will be my pleasure to lead you there."

Gomol was spun around, and with great deftness the other disarmed him. Gomol had carried two daggers, a short blade and a long, deadly one. Both were pitched far beyond a distant dune.

The Fashaar now faced his attacker for the first time, and he was surprised by what he saw. The fellow, from his looks and his garb, was definitely a Shadzean. It was rare to see one here, for the Kobur River was more than four days' ride to the west. He was a young man, Gomol saw, tall and well muscled. But there was a determination in his eyes, a hardness that far surpassed his relatively brief time in the world, and Gomol was glad that he had not challenged him further. He was most probably a bandit from one of Shadzea's far eastern provinces, Gomol reasoned, and had crossed over into the desert in search of quick riches. This desert nomad would have believed no one had he been told that he stood in the presence of a prince of Shadzea.

The grim young man retrieved his steed, and he ordered Gomol to mount his own. They set out together toward the north, Dulok staying well in back of his unwilling guide to avoid treachery. All that day they rode across the blistering sands, stopping infrequently. Gomol became exhausted, but he dared not complain. They stopped for the night shortly after sundown, when they dined on sweetmeats and water. Dulok bound Gomol's arms and legs as a precaution, but it would not have mattered, for the heavy man slept soundly through the night. At times his snoring disturbed the sleep of Dulok.

For three more days and nights they continued their trek, but the harsh, barren landscape of white sand went unchanged. Dulok had started out with a goodly supply of water, but over the last two days he had had to share it with Gomol, who possessed only a limited amount, since a long journey had not been in his plans. They had as yet sighted no water, and Gomol knew of none for many days, not until they neared the tents of Ibdan.

Once again the sun had begun to sink low, and soon they would halt their journey for the night. Dulok had chafed at the slow progress they made, but after one day he had realized that the weighty nomad could not maintain his own pace, and he slowed accordingly, lest he lose this valuable guide.

The top of a nearby desert palm suddenly became visible over a swirling dune. Dulok instructed Gomol to ride toward the tree, and the nomad's tired beast, sensing an end to the day's trek, scaled the mound of sand with ease. Dulok's own stallion, although unused to this hostile environment, nonetheless kept pace with the lead horse, and soon they had reached what they sought. The

100

visible palm was only one of a cluster, and all stood beside a small, shimmering pool of water.

"Look, fenda, at what we have found!" the excited Gomol shouted. "Surely Yhemi has smiled on us today. Hurry, fenda, so that we might drink our fill."

Dulok motioned Gomol toward the water, and he followed him slowly. There was an odd sensation here that made his skin prickle, but he did not understand why. The two stopped only yards from the edge of the pool, and Dulok held tightly to the reins of his horse, who otherwise would have strode to the water to drink. Gomol, after tethering his own steed, took an empty gourd from his bag and filled it full of the clear, shimmering liquid. He then offered it to Dulok.

"Drink, fenda, drink!" he grinned. "I offer you this gourd in friendship. Why should we continue to travel as enemies?"

But the sudden generosity of the oily Fashaar only served to heighten Dulok's questionable feelings about this strange oasis. He took the proferred drink from the smiling Gomol, but he did not put it to his lips. Instead, he looked at the nomad and grinned.

"You are right, my friend," he stated. "There is no need for us to quarrel. We *shall* be friends! And since we are friends, and I see that you perspire more freely than myself, I will let *you* take the first drink. In the name of friendship, of course!"

The broad grin lessened, but Gomol managed to retain his composure. "Oh no, fenda, the first drink shall be yours." He appeared to be pleading with the prince. "You will honor me by—!"

Dulok, weary of the game, thrust the gourd into the

Fashaar's hands and grabbed the collar of his begrimed robe. He lifted Gomol up, until his face had turned a pasty white and his tongue protruded from his mouth.

"Drink this water, Fashaar, *now!*" he ordered, and the quaking Gomol nodded vigorously. Dulok released him, and he watched the nomad lift the gourd to his lips. But before he took a sip his hands began to shake visibly, as if he bore some strange desert malady. Water flew from the gourd in all directions, some splashing upon the thin tunic of Dulok.

"Fenda, I cannot drink this water!" he shrieked. "Please, do not make me drink it!"

"Tell me why you will not drink this water!" Dulok snapped. "Hurry, before I pour it down your wretched throat, for I tire of your deceit!"

"This is the—the Oasis of Ghadi!" Gomol blurted. "To drink the water here is—to die! It is a forbidden place!"

"And you would have had me drink the water, you Fashaar cur, in the name of friendship!" Dulok struck the gourd from Gomol's hands and drew his sword. The fat man dropped to his knees, his body quaking in terror.

"Please, fenda!" he begged, tears pouring from his eyes. "In the name of Yhemi, do not kill me! I have two women, and seven small ones! I will lead you to the tents of Ibdan, and will cause you no further trouble, this I swear! Please, fenda, please!"

There was something in the pathetic, cringing figure that made Dulok stay his hand. His patience had grown infinitely shorter since the day, years past, that he had departed the City of Madness, but he still found the indiscriminate taking of a life to be distasteful. True, this fellow had tried to poison him, but only in defense of his own life. Would he himself not have done the same thing? Also, to be left alone without a destination in this accursed Desert of Craters was to invite death. He needed this Fashaar, and he begrudgingly sheathed his blade.

They rested that night in the shadow of the Oasis of Ghadi. The horses were watered from the precious stores, and were then tethered at some distance so as not to accidently partake of the poisoned well. Dulok allowed Gomol his share of food and water, but he himself sipped only a little. Once again the Fashaar's hands and feet were bound, and only when his gruff snoring broke the stillness of the desert did the prince himself chance sleep.

Dulok's eyes were opened wide, and a faint smile creased his lips. The two steeds were nowhere to be seen, but this did not register in the prince's brain. Instead, he watched torpidly as the bulky Gomol rose slowly to his feet. The bonds wrapped around his ankles had been snapped as if they were threads, and with a simple flick of the wrists he did the same to the ties that held his hands. A myriad of flickering stars shone down upon the silent desert as Gomol ambled slowly toward the pool. Dulok could not understand his purpose, but he nonetheless took amusement in the actions of the Fashaar.

The water in the small pool, clear and calm during the day, now undulated vigorously, like the waves of the Telliun Ocean. An eerie, bluish glow was visible from the depths of the pool, depths which Dulok might otherwise have thought minimal, but which now appeared to extend far down into the bowels of the earth.

Gomol reached the edge of the pool, where he stopped. He turned slowly, until he faced Dulok, and the blank

103

expression that he had worn was now replaced by a look that could only have indicated limitless, mind-wrenching terror. He opened his mouth to scream, but no sound emanated from his throat. He held his hands out to Dulok, as if in supplication; but Dulok sat frozen, the dull smile still masking his face.

The last thread of awareness had been snapped, and Gomol no longer was cognizant of Dulok. He stepped backward, until he stood in the center of the pool, in water apparently waist deep. The small, gently rolling waves now began to churn around him, and his body sank slowly, slowly, until only his head could be seen above the surface. The whites around his eyes showed clearly as they widened in horror, and, before the head vanished completely, the two orbs bulged forth from their sockets and disappeared into the murky depths of the pool.

Dulok rose to his feet and walked calmly toward the pool, which, with the disappearance of Gomol, had quieted again. Now it was as still as it had been when he first set eyes on it that afternoon. The water looked clear and inviting, surely the ideal balm to soothe a parched throat. Gomol's empty gourd lay at his feet, and he scooped it up so that he might easily partake of the refreshment. He bent over and dipped the gourd into the water, and with an expression of delight he lifted it to his lips. . . .

The water's hue altered once again, and it began to churn vigorously, as if great fires had been lighted beneath it. Dulok, the gourd inches from his lips, paused to stare in wonder at the incandescent pool, and what he witnessed served to return the spark of consciousness to him that temporarily stayed his death. A figure was spewed forth from the pool, rising taller than even

Dulok. As he gazed above him, the young prince saw two pits staring out into the desert night, holes where once there had been eyes. The blackened death's-head sat atop a charred, mouldering body, all that remained of he who had once been Gomol, the Fashaar!

Dulok, far stronger of will than the superstitious nomad, had not initially been fully overcome by the forces of this unholy place, or he too would have docilely strolled to his death in the terrible pool. Now, as he shook the remaining lethargy from his fogged brain, he saw that he had nearly poisoned himself. He cast away the gourd, disgusted for his weakness. He wanted to flee from this foul place, but his legs would not respond to his will.

The water from the pool continued to spurt skyward as he felt his legs for signs of paralysis. He was suddenly felled by a crushing blow, and for moments he lay there, stunned. A weighty object pressed down upon him, and he reached up to push it off with his hands. But as he gripped the object tightly he felt a slimy ooze seep through his fingers, and when he glanced upward he saw that he held the rotting, fetid flesh of Gomol's corpse. He screamed as he cast the foul thing from him, not noticing that it again sank into the depths of the pool from where it had spewed forth. He rose to his feet and ran blindly into the desert, not even stopping to gather his meager stores. That his legs again functioned was a fact that he failed to notice, nor did he care. To leave this accursed Oasis of Ghadi was the thought that dominated his tormented brain.

For hours Dulok staggered through the still desert, until his fatigue overwhelmed him, and he crumpled in a heap upon the sand. He slept fitfully, his slumber troubled by nightmares, visions of horrors he had encountered in his lifetime, and ones he had not. Only when the fiery orb that marked the passage of day began to sear his exposed flesh did he awaken. He shook the fog from his head as he looked about him, for he did not know how he had gotten there, nor did he at first recall what had transpired. The horses were gone, as was Gomol! He remembered the Fashaar, and he knew that what had occurred at the Oasis of Ghadi was no nightmare, but a real and incomprehensible thing. He shuddered as he thought of the fate of the obese nomad. True, the death of one turbaned rogue meant nothing to him, but even a Fashaar should not have to meet a death as cruel and horrible as that.

The young prince shook these thoughts from his mind, for he knew that his dilemma was of more immediate concern. He had no horse, no water, and no guide. In this searing desert there might not be water for hundreds of miles around him. Then again, he might pass within yards of the precious fluid and not even be aware of its presence. He did not know in which direction he had fled the Oasis of Ghadi, but it was a simple enough matter to direct himself north. There he would find the tents of Ibdan, and perhaps the object of his search. But how far was it to Ibdan's seikhdom? Ten miles? Twenty? Maybe one hundred! He knew that he could not last for any length of time under the blazing sun, but his choices were limited. With a shrug of his shoulders he began his plodding journey to an unknown fate.

The wicked sun rose higher, while the spirits of Dulok slowly ebbed. All that day he strode across the burning sand as if in a drug-induced trance. He freed his mind from all thoughts, lest he should weaken and fall, and he prayed to his distant gods, who eventually rewarded him.

A small desert lizard scurried under his feet, and with a blinding motion he thought himself incapable of he snatched it up. He devoured whatever flesh he could find on the small creature, and sucked its juices dry. The meager repast gave him new strength, along with renewed hope.

The sun sank rapidly, and the desert air became cool, but Dulok continued on for hours. In those few hours he traveled more miles than he had during the entire day. However, his great fatigue and insatiable thirst again overcame him, and he begrudgingly conceded. He lay quietly on the cool sand, at first unable to sleep, and he contemplated the ill fortune that had led him to this spot. He might survive the next day, and even that was questionable. Beyond that, he knew that his fate had been all but sealed. The merciless Desert of Craters would crush to its bosom another insignificant cairn of bleached bones. The death of Daynea would go unavenged, and the gentle Sallia would belong to Buz, in which case Dulok knew that the poor girl would take her own life.

Dulok fell asleep with these dispiriting thoughts pressing upon him, and once again his slumber was restless, but not so much as the night before. He awakened before dawn and continued the trek north, and for the first hour, before the appearance of the sun, his spirits soared. But soon the blazing ball, benevolent giver of light and warmth, had again begun to pour its fire down upon this cruel Desert of Craters. By mid-morning Dulok had fallen to his hands and knees, and he crawled along the heated sand pitifully, his parched tongue protruding from between cracked lips.

He heard a sound in the midst of the still desert, which

at first he attributed to the caprices of an addled brain. But again he heard it, and then a third time. It was nearby, and it was unmistakable: the gentle whinny of a horse! With a new strength that had been contained deep within him, he forced himself to his feet and hurriedly climbed the dune that stood between him and the source of the sound. From atop the hill of sand he gazed downward, and with his dried lips he managed to force a meager smile, for there he saw his own black stallion, as well as the mount of Gomol. Both stood calmly at the edge of a tiny water hole!

The elated prince moved slowly toward the pool, so as not to frighten the two steeds. He need not have worried about his own horse, for, once over its shock from the incident at the Oasis of Ghadi, it had searched vainly for its master, and was now joyed to see him. The other horse, without guidance, had stayed close to the stallion, and chose not to leave. Dulok spoke softly to each horse for a moment, after which he satisfied his great thirst. His own water pouch had been left behind, but the pouch of Gomol still remained on his horse, and Dulok finished the tiny amount that was left. Still thirsty, he gazed suspiciously at the small well, fearful to partake of it. But soon he realized that the contented horses must have drank their fill, and they still lived. He cupped his hands and cautiously tasted the water. Though slightly brackish it was nonetheless life-giving, precious water, and as he splashed it over his face and body the young prince knew that his prayers had not been ignored.

Dulok tethered both steeds, and from the materials contained in the saddle pouches of each he constructed a rude shelter, where the three were protected from the scorching sun for the remainder of that day. The next morning he filled all the available water bags to the top, and with the Fashaar's horse in tow he set out for the seikhdom of Ibdan. His hope renewed, he felt confident over the potential success of this quest, his Trial of Death.

CHAPTER EIGHT

THE TENTS OF IBDAN

It had taken three more days of harsh travel, but Dulok now knew that he had reached the seikhdom of Ibdan. Oases were more numerous, and for the first time there was livestock, sturdy desert goats that bleated loudly under the nonstop berating of the herdsmen. More Fashaars were to be seen also. At first Dulok had concealed himself when any neared, but soon he realized that they were, like him, merely travelers. With garments he had acquired from a merchants' caravan in exchange for Gomol's horse, the prince was able to shield his identity and meld with the others. Had it not been for the fine animal that he rode, no one would have afforded him a second look.

Another day's ride through the only fertile lands he had seen here brought Dulok to the edge of a vast, craterlike depression, one of the many that gave this desert its name. He saw trees the like of which were unknown to him, and they bore many strange, exotic fruits. He had sampled some, and found them to be delectable. Heavily irrigated fields sprouted grains, as well as other fruits and vegetables. He understood now how these Fashaars could survive in this hostile land, and why Ibdan, whose rule extended over this territory, was as powerful as Gomol thought him to be.

From his position at the edge of the depression, Dulok peered down at a wonderous sight. In the distant center of the crater was a sea of brightly colored tents, stretching for miles in all directions. But in the middle of this desert city a singular tent stood out, even from such a distance. It was far larger than the rest, and the acres of empty ground that surrounded it told of the caution taken by its occupant. That this was the tent of Ibdan himself, and perhaps the end of his quest, Dulok had no doubt.

Various crudely carved trails led downward into the crater, and all were well guarded. The chance of any vast contingent approaching this city undetected was nil. Dulok feared close scrutiny by the guards along the trail he chose, lest his western appearance give him away. As a precaution he patiently awaited an arriving caravan, and as one of the many obscure lackeys he easily made his way into the city.

Not forgetting his purpose for an instant, Dulok nevertheless took time to wonder at the strange way of life of these desert dwellers. As he led his horse along the dusty streets, he saw numerous vendors hawking unfamiliar wares from distant places. Sultry beauties in thin, flowing garments drew travelers into their tents of pleasure with the alluring tinkle of tiny bells, which they wore on the fingers of their beckoning hands. Ill-tempered, humped beasts spat menacingly at potential purchasers. Aged beggars moaned pathetically in the dust, while obnoxious children hurled stones and taunts

111

at them. The ways of the Fashaars were indeed an enigma to this son of Shadzea, born of royalty and taught in the ways of his people.

After nearing the center of the city, Dulok left his fine steed loosely tethered to a railing in front of an inn. He had long discarded anything that could identify him as other than a simple Fashaar traveler, and he was unconcerned lest the horse be examined. From the edge of the inner circle of city tents he gazed across the open area at the tent of the seikh, and he knew that his task would be more difficult than he had first imagined. Numerous guards stalked the grounds between the city and the seikh's tent, and their cruel, hawklike visages foretold of great punishment in store for those who might choose to test them. Even under the cover of darkness it might prove no mean feat to bypass these villains.

Dulok continued to move about, so as not to be noticed in one spot for any length of time. Once he saw a procession of about eight men, under the leadership of a scowling, barking overseer, cross the area to the tent unchallenged. They returned to the city, and minutes later the scene was repeated. Each man carried a platter heaped with fruits, meat, and other delicacies. Dulok had moved closer to their point of departure, apparently a kitchen tent, and before they were too far away he managed to catch some of the overseer's words.

". . . of guests, and lots of guests require lots of food! Be careful, fools! Do not drop a thing, or Ibdan will have all our heads. You there—!"

His words became unintelligible, but Dulok had learned what he wanted. The guards again paid no heed to this procession, evidently the caterers to some great feast

112

that Ibdan was providing. Would they be making another trip? He peered cautiously into the kitchen, and the numerous trays told him that this was a certainty.

The group returned once more, grabbed their respective trays, and repeated their march across the grounds. When the last one had departed the tent, Dulok entered. He snatched a tray of fruits and exited the tent, but only after making certain that his hood more than adequately concealed his face. With a few long strides he attached himself to the end of the line. The guards paid him little mind, for it was unlikely that they were counting, and less probable that any could even tally.

The overseer, still shouting invectives at his charges, held open the flap on the rear of the main tent so that all might enter with little risk of spilling his tray. Each received his own personal imprecation as he passed, including Dulok, whom the foul-tempered fellow seemed to acknowledge as one of his lackeys. Dulok sighed deeply at this stroke of good fortune.

Once inside, the overseer led the group through a maze of gauze and canvas, until they reached the main feasting area of Ibdan's tent. The trays were deposited on the rug-covered floor amidst the many that were already there, and the path back through the tent was again taken. But the party left with one less, for Dulok had managed to break away and conceal himself behind a rich, finely woven tapestry that covered one wall of the spacious area. He waited there until he was certain the room had been vacated, and he then emerged.

His first interest was a more advantageous place to hide, but he could discover none as promising as the one he had first utilized. He then scanned the area for any clue to the whereabouts of the Stone of Bao, though he quickly realized the futility of such an action. If the stone was indeed in the possession of Ibdan, it would surely be under heavy guard. He would force this Ibdan to turn over the jewel, assuming that he could locate the seikh's quarters. Perhaps the corridor he had first come through . . .

A distant noise sent him scampering back to the safety of the thick tapestry. He waited, hardly daring to breathe. Once again the ill-tempered overseer and his kitchen lackeys entered. There had only been a few trays left when Dulok took his, and he was certain that this would be their last trip. The words of the overseer affirmed this.

"How fortunate we are, you dogs!" he snapped. "Despite your laziness we have still managed to deliver our wares in time for the seikh's feast. Return to the kitchen now, lest he find us lolling here and have us boiled for it!"

The grumbling party filed out, and Dulok was glad to have seen the last of them. Again he would have left his place of concealment, but a faint tinkling of bells froze him where he stood. The sound grew louder, and soon he knew that others occupied the room.

"Where will Ibdan be seated?" a female voice spoke.

"Where else, foolish Jhaata, than the largest chair in the room?" replied another teasingly. "See! It is the one on the far wall. What other chair do you see in which he can fit?"

"Weesha!" a third voice snapped. "You should know better than to talk like that here! In the tents of Ibdan, even the canvas listens!"

"Keliin is right, Weesha," offered Jhaata. "And

114

besides, the seikh has bedded me numerous times. I assure you, his bulk belies his agility."

The three giggled unashamedly, while Dulok felt the blood rush to his face. He listened to the tinkling of the bells and the soft singing of the girls as they made ready for the feast. After much preparation Dulok heard another, more authoritative voice in the hall.

"Has nothing gotten done yet?" the voice lisped. "They will soon be here!" The tone was husky, yet effeminate.

"Be calm, sweet Peelik," laughed the one called Keliin. "We are done. But what of yourself? You'd best be gone from here before they arrive, lest you find yourself enamored of one of the northern seikhs. We understand that those of the north have devised delectable tortures for ones such as you!"

The girls laughed heartily, while Peelik fumed. "Daughter of a camel!" he screeched. "Skinny slut! What Ibdan sees in you is unknown to me. You are a— a—!"

"Oh, never mind, Peelik," Weesha chuckled gaily. "Listen! They come! Let us be ready to serve them."

Dulok heard much uproarious laughter. First it came from afar, but soon it resounded through the hall he occupied, and the large room reeked with the odor of the many bodies that filled it. Through a tiny flaw in the tapestry, Dulok managed to view the proceedings. Swarthy, bearded Fashaars swarmed throughout, each opulently bedecked in jewels and other ornaments, as befitting their positions. But none was so adorned as the figure that occupied the great chair, an obese fellow who himself appeared to be hewn from jewels. One could scarce look at him without squinting his eyes. A quartet of sensual concubines fawned over the repulsive body of Ibdan, the most powerful seikh in the Desert of Craters.

"My friends, be silent!" Ibdan roared. The hall became as a tomb. "I welcome the seikhs of the north and the east," he continued. "This feast is in your honor, and as such, anything you desire is yours. There is plenty of food to go around, and more than enough women. And if one does not suffice you, let your friend Ibdan know. He will see to it you are given all you can handle, and perhaps more!"

The others chortled uproariously at the seikh's words, and the great feast began. There was much talk, much laughter, and a variety of entertainment. The Fashaars ate and drank with gusto, and their pleasure was indicated by the thunderous belches that emanated from the depths of their sated bellies. The disgusted Dulok chafed at the length of the feast, but he had no other choice than to remain where he was, for he knew that an appearance would precipitate a shower of Fashaar daggers, all of which would doubtless find a place of rest in or near his heart.

The overstuffed seikhs reclined in various obscene positions, while the remains of their repast was cleared away. Ibdan again silenced the hall, for he had an announcement to make.

"I have a surprise for all of you!" he told them. His meaty hands clapped together twice, and a luscious concubine appeared, a flat velvet box in her hands. The seikh snatched the receptacle, and he continued: "I purchased this item only recently from two brave thieves, fine sons of Yhemi. They stole this from under

116

the noses of the accursed red priests of Shadzea, in the City of Gods. Behold, my brothers, the Stone of Bao!"

Ibdan held the amulet high for all to see, and the others gasped in amazement at its splendor. To own this treasure was indeed the right of a powerful seikh such as Ibdan, and all came forward to gaze upon it. But none could have been more thankful for its presence than the hungry, fatigued young prince of Shadzea who stood stiffly behind the tapestry. His long, nearly fatal search had at last led him to the right place, and he thanked the gods for their guidance.

The interminable banquet went forth, and the fiery date liquor of the desert flowed as swiftly and as freely as an ocean current. Soft, perfumed concubines were as plentiful as the drink, and the spacious hall in the tent of Ibdan became a scene of unimagined debauchery. On numerous occasions the revellers came within inches of crashing into the tapestry, which surely would have given Dulok away. But fortune was still with the young prince, and after countless hours the orgy had all but ended. Dulok peered through the opening in the tapestry, noting that everyone, both seikhs and women, lay unclothed on the floor in various obscene positions, all in one form or another of drunken stupor. Most notable among them was the gross body of Ibdan, who snored loudly on his chair, while four slumbering concubines lounged at his feet. Only one item adorned his repulsive flesh, a brilliant amulet that depended from his neck; the Stone of Bao!

Dulok quitted his hiding place and cautiously made his way across the hall, deftly sidestepping the prostrated bodies on the floor. He came up behind the chair of

Ibdan, and with great care he began removing the necklace from the sweaty body. Slowly, slowly he brought it up over the head, until it was free of the Fashaar who had wrongfully possessed it. He clutched it tightly in his hand for a moment, and once more the vengeance of Daynea was nearer.

Ibdan suddenly scowled and snorted, as if from a bad dream. He thrust his foot forward, and one of the concubines toppled over with a thud. This sleek beauty, jarred from her sleep, opened her eyes, and at the sight of Dulok perpetrating his theft she screamed. Instantly the hall of Ibdan became a place of bedlam as seikhs and females, rudely awakened, rose groggily to their feet and scurried about aimlessly. The women screamed, while the Fashaars, who cursed loudly and would have drawn daggers, found themselves as weaponless as they were unclothed.

In the ensuing confusion, Dulok raced across the hall to a flap in the tent that he was certain would lead him to freedom. Many stunned seikhs were unceremoniously bowled over in his frantic flight. Ibdan, one of the first to regain his senses, noted the missing jewel, and he began to scream commands to all within his sphere.

"He stole the amulet! Stop him, you dogs!" he shrieked. "Stop him, or I will have the skin flayed from your hides! I will have your ears fed to the camels! I will—!"

Dulok heard no more of Ibdan's vile epithets, for he now raced across the open area that separated the tent of Ibdan from the remainder of the city that encircled it. It was night, but just how late Dulok could not tell, for his sojourn in the tent had been interminable. At first he was not noticed, and he felt that he might have a chance of bypassing the guards and reaching the city. But as he looked back he saw the opening of Ibdan's tent disgorge a dozen naked, swearing seikhs, and had it not been for his tenuous position, Dulok might have found the sight amusing.

"May Yhemi take all your black souls!" screeched Ibdan, who led the procession from the tent. "Where are my worthless guards? This dog must be stopped! A gold coin to the one who brings him to me!"

The guards, who had most likely been shirking their duties in light of the seikh's feast, suddenly appeared from everywhere, and Dulok's path to the city was cut off. He veered away and tried another, but the guards had begun to draw a net tightly around him. Knowing that he was surrounded, the prince raised his fingers to his mouth and sounded a sharp, piercing whistle, a signal he had taught his fine steed many years before, when it was a colt. The patient horse heard his master's call, and he easily broke the light tether that Dulok had tied, anticipating just such an emergency.

The guards approached the intruder slowly and cautiously, for all had imbibed a bit that evening, and their heads were not yet clear. Suddenly a great and terrible engine of destruction broke through their ranks, and before any knew what had occurred, Dulok's powerful stallion had reduced their number on its unerring path to heed its master's call. Two Fashaars lay dead, three others injured and bleeding in the dust.

Dulok hastily launched himself onto the stallion's back, and with little break in stride the horse rode onward, into another cluster of guards. This time the Fashaars spread apart to allow the formidable creature egress, but still another was trampled beneath the hooves

119

of the beast, and two others were hurt. Dulok guided the horse into the city, where they quickly vanished from the sight of Ibdan.

"To your mounts, scum!" The seikh's voice reached Dulok even in the city. "Ten pieces of gold to the one who brings the devil to me! Hurry, dogs, or I will see to it that your further service to Ibdan is carried out in the dung heaps of the stables!"

Dulok raced his steed between the clusters of tents, and anyone who chanced to stray into their path suffered appropriate injury. At breakneck speed it required but minutes to exit the city, and now only the vast, open floor of the crater remained between Dulok and the closest trail that led to safety above. He knew he would encounter resistance, but he was determined that nothing would bar his escape from this accursed place, now that he had retrieved what he had come for.

A loud gong was sounded in the core of the tent city, and its echoes reverberated throughout the crater. Dulok, certain that this was a signal, urged his stallion just a bit harder. He chanced a quick look to his rear, and he saw that anyone who had access to a mount rode in pursuit of him. All were just emerging onto the plain. Some even rode the strange beasts that he believed to be called camels, but these ungainly animals offered no challenge to his steed.

The first twisting trail loomed only a quarter of a mile ahead, but in the moonlight Dulok could see that no less than five mounted Fashaars stood sentry at its base. Still he bore down upon them, hoping that the daring tactic would cause them uncertainty. But these guards had not partaken of any heady spirits that night, and the signal from the city had alerted them. Their curved swords were drawn, and Dulok saw that he would be forced into battle with them if he hoped to gain access to the trail.

Years of intense, vigorous training as a prince of Shadzea were now tested to the fullest as the lone rider, his lengthy sword drawn, forged his way into the heart of the quintet. Like a desert whirlwind he hewed through their ranks, and before any of them realized what they had come up against, the adept warrior had already lessened their number. One fell heavily to the dust, only the most fragile piece of flesh holding the nearly severed head to the remainder of the body; a second stood tall atop his steed, a look of disbelief on his face, and watched his own life escape through a crimson hole in his chest.

The three remaining Fashaars backed away, all most wary and quite in awe of this formidable swordsman. The initial advantage had been his, but Dulok knew that dispatching the rest would not be as simple. The guards fanned out and guided their horses slowly toward the fiery, panting stallion. Dulok, aware of the purpose of this tactic, backed his steed away, though he never once lowered his sword. It was this menacing blade that kept the Fashaars at a safe distance.

The thunder of many hooves sounded closer. Dulok dared not look behind him, but he knew that the legions of Ibdan were closing quickly. He would have to make a move now, or it would be all for naught. He drove his heels into the sides of the stallion and bore down upon the Fashaar furthest to his left. Before the fellow had a chance to react he found himself gazing at his own sword arm, which now lay in the dust at his mount's feet, the sword still clutched tightly between nerveless fingers. The others turned their animals to cut him off, but he utilized the stallion's speed in describing a wide arc around them. Now there were less than twenty-five yards before he would ascend the winding trail to safety above.

The gods of Shadzea chose a strange time to desert their son, the fearless prince whom they had brought so far. But desert him they did, for neither horse nor rider saw the burrow of a small animal directly in their path. For only an instant the foot of the fine beast stuck in the hole, but it was enough to buckle the steed and send Dulok hurtling forward, where he fell with great force amidst a clump of rocks. He was momentarily stunned, and the two guards, who had been close at his heels, now pounced on him and easily disarmed him. They pinioned his arms tightly and held him there, just as the irate Ibdan and his force arrived.

"You western dog!" roared Ibdan, for with the removal of Dulok's robes his identity became clear. "You dare to defile the tent of Ibdan with your thievery! I will have your flesh cut into tiny morsels for the curs to eat! I will have you staked under the desert sun, until you pray for the sting of the scorpion to end your wretched life!"

He paused to catch his breath, looking closely at Dulok to see what effect his threats had. But Dulok remained impassive, and the seikh continued to rage.

"A hundred pieces of gold to the one who can devise a fitting punishment for this believer of false gods!" he bellowed to those around him.

At once the suggestions began to fly, and the description of each torture far exceeded the one that had preceded it. Ibdan listened to each one with great pleasure, pausing only briefly to order one of the guards to fetch the Stone of Bao from Dulok. He lovingly caressed the amulet with his thick fingers, and he grinned broadly as it once again hung about his neck.

Suddenly this moody seikh began to tire of the tumult, and he motioned all to silence. He looked about thoughtfully, and all awaited his decision.

"What of you, Hameel?" he said, indicating one of the seikhs who had been among his guests. "We have not heard from you. Surely a great northern seikh would have something to say in this matter."

This scowling old seikh gazed upon Dulok, and he then faced his host. "My dear friend Ibdan," he hissed. "The imagination of a Fashaar is indeed vivid. Never before have I heard such delectable tortures. But were he made to suffer for an hour, five hours, even a day, it would not be long enough to atone for the heinous act he has perpetrated here. His punishment must be of considerable duration."

"And your suggestion, Hameel?" Ibdan asked. "Quickly, for I weary of this!"

"The northern mines, my seikh," he stated simply.

"The mines!" Ibdan roared. "How perfect! Month after month his torment will linger, even year after year if he is strong enough. I can even come to observe his suffering, as it pleases me. Well done, Hameel; the gold is yours!"

The minions cheered lustily at the pleasure of their leader, while Dulok struggled in vain against the numerous Fashaars who now held him. He was returned to the city, where he spent the cold night under heavy guard. No food or water was brought to him, and his hands and feet were tightly bound.

The next morning Dulok departed the crater that housed the tents of Ibdan, but not in the manner he would have chosen. He was a prisoner in a caravan under the leadership of Hameel, and he was forced to walk, for his fine stallion had been confiscated for the personal use of Ibdan. What unspeakable tortures lay to the north was unknown to him, but his limited experience with the Fashaars assured him that it would not be to his liking.

CHAPTER NINE

ACROSS THE RIVER

More than six months had passed since Dulok first departed the City of Kings, but still he had not returned. Those who were concerned with his life sent messenger hawks to the City of Gods often, only to repeatedly find that the Stone of Bao had not been re-enshrined by the one who sought it. All knew that much time still remained for the successful completion of his trial, but six months seemed like an eternity to them, especially Sallia. She spent most of her days watching the road that led to the main gate, and at times her vigil was joined by Qual.

"I fear for him, Qual, and each day he is gone I fear for him more," Sallia stated one day, as the long afternoon ended in another depressing sunset.

"I feel no different than you, my dear," the faithful mentor replied. "I have been with Dulok since he was eight years of age, and to me he is like a son. Were he of simple birth, and not the seed of Ornon, I would care for him no less."

"My feelings for him are the same," Sallia admitted.

"Often I've cursed the fates that have made us what we are. At times I believe that Dulok feels no differently, yet he is one of the Twenty, and as such he must continue in order to survive. What could make him like this, beyond the will to live? Together we could leave the city and live in peace in some obscure province. Many times I have thought of asking him, but I check myself."

"As a child, Dulok appeared to show little interest in the prospect of becoming the fifteenth Survivor," Qual related. "I thought surely that he would not grow to manhood. Only his great natural skills and strength kept him alive. But then he changed; I cannot remember when it was, perhaps three or four years after he came to me. No matter, for practically overnight a change was wrought in him. A grim determination heretofore absent suddenly appeared, and I knew that it was his desire to survive until the end. I have done everything I could to help him achieve that goal, but only because it was his wish, and not the will of Ornon."

"But what could have happened to change him?" Sallia asked.

"This I do not know," Qual shrugged, "and I doubt if anyone other than Dulok does. But I can tell you this: since he has met you, he has changed even more. Often he appears wistful, and he is torn between whatever it is that impels him and his love for you. He himself wonders at the comparative importance of the former. This he has never told me, but I know."

"I love him dearly, Qual," Sallia confided. "But I would never ask him to give up what he seeks for me. Perhaps some day we shall know."

So continued the vigil of the two, while in other rooms of the palace there were those who also had an interest in the fate of Dulok. Most would have been glad not to see his face ever again; but one, who despised him beyond the imagination of all, wished him a horrible death, and would have been pleased to observe the wretched remains of his body.

There was another in the palace whose interest in Dulok had begun to dwindle as the months passed. Ornon, for the first time in many years, doubted his own feelings about the desire to see Buz as his heir. His other three sons had long since departed on their Trials of Death, and rumor had it that Korb was even now returning to the City of Fishers with the carcass of the zkreel he had sworn to destroy. But the first son still lingered in the palace, and as yet had not given any indication regarding the nature of his trial.

"Your procrastination troubles me, Buz," Ornon informed his son one day. "The people talk. You must embark on your Trial of Death soon, for the time passes rapidly."

"The Trial of Death that I choose will be one to be remembered by all of Shadzea, my father," Buz advised him. "As yet such a task has not arisen, but I feel that one day soon this will change. Fear not, for you will not be embarrassed; not by me!"

And Ornon chose to believe Buz, for he found it difficult to doubt him, his first son, the only son conceived out of passion.

In eternal darkness one could not accurately judge the passage of time, much less the night or the day. One could only try and remember how often he had slept since his arrival. Dulok had tried to maintain a count, but he had found it to be impossible, for his mind had often

127

been torn by the wracking labors he had endured. That he had slept hundreds of times was a certainty, since it was the sole thing to do when not at work.

From the first he had borne the burden of heavy manacles, both on his wrists and ankles. Under the vicious, stinging whip of a cruel Fashaar overseer he would trudge wearily, over and over, into the bowels of the earth. He would gather weighty chunks of crude ore in two wooden receptacles, which he would then drape over his shoulders with thick hemp. The burns from the rope dug deeply into his back, and were often as painful as the senseless whippings he endured.

But this prince of Shadzea had not accepted his hopeless situation with total resignation. Unbeknownst to his cruel taskmasters, he managed to steal a small piece of metal from the site of the digging, which he concealed under the dirt of his sleeping place. He purposely remained apart from those poor souls who shared his burdens, and hour after excruciating hour he would file the chains on his ankles. Even so, numerous sleeps had come and gone before even a nick could be discerned in the metal.

The endless hours in the mine dragged on, and often Dulok felt the urge to surrender to his situation; but the flames of survival, fueled by the antithetical emotions of love and hatred, sustained him. Slowly, slowly he wore through the thick metal, until the time came when he was certain that a simple snap would free his legs. But he waited, for he knew that the time was not right, and he also knew that any abortive attempt at escape would only win him heavier chains and a fleshless back.

Rumors had spread through the shafts for days that Ibdan, greatest seikh among the Fashaars, would inspect this mine, surely his most productive, within days. No one could perceive that this rumor had any connection with the sudden mental collapse of one of their better laborers, a westerner. When at rest, this poor soul would stare blankly at the walls and mumble unintelligibly, much to the amusement of the heartless Fashaars. He still functioned at his tasks, although additional prodding was sometimes necessary.

The day for the seikh's visit arrived, and the Fashaars saw to it that all was in readiness. The crazed westerner, who enjoyed a rest period at the time of the seikh's arrival, was hidden in an unused shaft, so as not to offend Ibdan. How amazed they all were when the seikh ordered them to show him this westerner, so that he might take pleasure in his suffering.

Hameel, the northern seikh, led Ibdan into the shaft, which barely allowed ingress to his great bulk. There, in a corner, lay the poor soul. His face was blank, and he uttered strange sounds.

"So here is the dog who would steal the Stone of Bao from Ibdan," grinned the seikh wickedly. "He has become a mindless, soulless creature. Your suggestion was indeed a worthy one, Hameel."

"Your words honor me, great Ibdan," said the oily Hameel.

"*No! No-o-o-o! Take it away! It is horrible!*" The creature on the floor was raving. "Look at it. Is it not beautiful? It—*No-o-o-o! Take it away . . . !*"

The voice dropped lower and lower, but the rantings continued. Ibdan was pleased by what he was seeing.

"Listen to him, Hameel," he laughed. "This indeed is a punishment befitting the crime. But what is he saying now? Something about accursed Shadzea? I cannot hear

129

him. I must get closer."

"Be careful, great seikh," Hameel warned. "One never knows just how dangerous such a madman can be."

"Do not be a fool, Hameel!" snapped Ibdan as he bent over the writhing body to better hear the utterings. "He is well chained, and besides—*aaiiyeee!*"

Ibdan's last scream was quickly stifled by the heavy chain that tightened around his neck. In a blurring, catlike motion Dulok had snapped the manacles on his ankles and leaped to his feet, promptly making Ibdan his prisoner. Hameel and two guards rushed forward, but Dulok tightened the chain around the terrified seikh's throat.

"Another step and this dog will breathe his last!" snapped Dulok, as Ibdan's flesh whitened. The trio halted. "You, Hameel! Have the tunnels that lead to the surface vacated. Make sure that you acquire the key to these cursed manacles from the overseer. Bring two steeds, the swiftest you have, to the entrance. See that I am provided with arms. I wish a longsword, not one of your useless curved pieces. Also, see that there is food, and much water; and rope! The seikh and I will ride out together, and no one will follow. Is that not the way it will be, Fashaar? Tell them!"

Dulok again tightened the chain, and Ibdan's eyes nearly bulged from their sockets. "It—it will be as he says!" the seikh gasped. "Hameel! Everything he has ordered will be carried out. Do not fail me!"

Hameel nodded grimly, and he motioned the guards out of the shaft.

"Wh-what will you do with me?" asked the terrified Ibdan as they waited. But Dulok chose to remain silent, and this only increased the terror of the cringing

Fashaar. "Spare me, and I will see to it that you have anything you desire. You wish the Stone of Bao? It is yours. Here, I have it upon my—*aahh!*"

Ibdan had gone to reach for the jewel, but Dulok viciously tightened the chain once again. "I will take from you what I wish, when I wish it, *Fashaar!*" he snapped, as he pulled the amulet from the seikh's neck and tucked it in the folds of his tattered breechcloth. "And if I wish your putrid life, I will take that also."

The Shadzean prince shoved his captive forward, and they traversed the tunnels to the surface. The sunlight nearly blinded Dulok, for it had been an eternity since he had seen the light of day; but his eyes adjusted quickly, and Ibdan never knew of his brief advantage. No Fashaar stood within fifty feet of the entrance save Hameel, who held the reins of two fine mounts. One was Dulok's own stallion, which Ibdan had used for himself since the westerner's capture. The beast, aware of his beloved master's presence, snorted happily, while Dulok motioned Hameel away so that he might share a moment of reunion with it.

"The weapons you asked for have been placed on this other steed—" Hameel began.

"Have them put on *my* horse," Dulok ordered. "Here is another possession I would regain from Ibdan."

Hameel did as he was told, and after handing Dulok the key to the chains he backed away. The prince drew the hefty sword and examined it, noting that it was a fine weapon. He placed the tip into Ibdan's back and motioned him to mount. Only after he sat astride his own horse did he release the chain, but the sword remained in its menacing position. He unlocked the weighty manacles and viciously hurled them at the overseer, whom he saw

131

at the forefront of the crowd. The blow felled the cruel Fashaar, crushing his skull.

"Remember," Dulok shouted at Hameel. "At the first appearance of pursuit, I will leave his carcass in the sand for the lizards to nip at his flesh."

Ibdan shuddered at the thought of such a fate, and his eyes silently pleaded with his underling to obey the will of the westerner. The two rode forward, and in minutes they had lost sight of the mine. Dulok prayed that he would never be forced to endure the torment of such a place again.

The prince altered their direction slightly, until he was certain that they were riding west. They rode all that long day, Dulok noting that Ibdan's steed was as tireless as his own. Despite the searing heat Dulok rode tall atop his stallion, for his freedom, as well as the retrieval of the Stone of Bao, had given him new life, new hope. He need but return to the City of Kings, where one final obligation went unfulfilled. Only then would the anguish of a lifetime cease to churn within him.

Dulok and his captive rode for four days. They encountered no one, nor did the cloud of dust that denoted pursuit rise behind them. Ibdan remained in mortal fear of his captor, who chose to say little. But he found that as long as he obeyed the westerner's orders he was not harmed, and he did all he could to please. Once he even pointed out the site of a well, and he drank of it first to prove its purity.

The landscape began to alter drastically; the blowing sand had turned to hard, albeit dry earth. Wild shrubs appeared, first brownish, but soon a more living shade of light green. Dulok knew that moisture was drawn from somewhere to provide for these plants, and he was

132

certain that the river could not be far off.

It was mid-morning, the fifth day after leaving the mine. Dulok and Ibdan sat atop a tree-covered hillock and gazed down upon the broad, shimmering expanse that was the Kobur River. The prince smiled to himself, for the end of his journey was drawing nearer. He looked at Ibdan, and for the first time in days his expression frightened the seikh.

"We part company here, Fashaar," he stated firmly. "Dismount!"

Ibdan did as he was told, knowing that his life hung in the balance.

"Turn around and begin walking back the way we came," Dulok ordered.

"In the name of Yhemi!" the seikh pleaded. "You would send me into the desert with no steed?"

"Leave quickly, before my patience thins!" snapped the prince.

"But, fenda, surely you would allow me a pouch of water!" Ibdan cried.

"I would think little of skewering you right here, Fashaar!" spat Dulok, who was quickly tiring of the seikh's presence. "That I grant you your life is enough, for it is more than you would do for me."

Dulok guided his steed down the hillock, the other animal held closely behind. Ibdan stood at the top and watched incredulously as the prince neared the bank of the river. He shuddered at the thought of what lay ahead of him, and he implored Yhemi to send his men to find him, before his bones littered the landscape of the Desert of Craters. He turned to leave, but realized that by manufacturing a receptacle he could carry away some of the river water with him into the desert, perhaps enough

133

to sustain him until he reached a well, or until he was found. He began his descent to the river, when suddenly he noticed Dulok and the two horses. They had entered the river, and already the gently flowing water reached nearly to the haunches of the beasts. Ibdan, feeling safe enough to scoff at his erstwhile captor with impunity, shouted after him.

"Westerner!" he screamed, and he saw Dulok's head turn toward him. "You go across the river?" It was more of a taunt than a question.

"You have eyes, do you not, Fashaar?" Dulok answered. "What of it to you?"

"You see the dense trees there in the distance?" Ibdan mocked. "Are you not aware of what you enter? Even Yhemi does not know what lies beyond those trees, for such is above the ken of even a god!"

"Then your god is weak," shouted Dulok, "as are the people he embraces!"

Dulok turned and urged his stallion onward into the deeper water, for his exchange with Ibdan was at an end. The seikh arrived at the edge of the river, where he stood and laughed at this foolish westerner. Dulok reached the sloping bank on the other side of the Kobur and topped it. He halted for a moment and contemplated the trees, which he too had seen from the opposite shore. He knew what he was about to do but without further pause for thought he plunged into the dense foliage. The echoes of Ibdan's laughter faded in the distance.

Dulok had been gone for more than seven months, and the will of the troubled Sallia appeared to be weakening daily. Buz, who still was to be found in the palace preparing for his fourth Princes' Trial, came to see her as often as possible, as was his right. But somehow he seemed different to her. He had acquired a new charm, a new tact, even humility. At first she had shunned him, for he had always been repulsive to her. But the lonesome girl sought a kind word, a smiling face, one of her own age. Buz sympathized with her at her grief, and initially he offered her many assurances that her lover would return. Eventually she came to trust and confide in him. It was then that Buz began to express his fears that the twentieth son was dead. Sallia at first refused to believe him, but his kindly manner offered no hint of purposeful deception.

Sallia's beauty had grown beyond compare, even in the time that Dulok had been gone. Buz was obsessed with the thought of possessing her, and during the playing of his lengthy game he had been forced to restrain himself to a degree that he had thought impossible. But now, unable to control himself any longer, he made numerous overtures to Sallia. He swore his great love for her, and he told her what it would be like as queen of Shadzea. Why waste such a young life, he had reasoned, loving a memory? She need not love him now, but later, perhaps, her love would grow.

The gentle Sallia listened, and at times she wavered; but she remembered Dulok's words, and she knew that she must never doubt them. She also recalled her own words, that she would not choose to live without him, and she knew that this was truly how she felt. She rejected all the advances of Buz, and the first son appeared to accept his defeat gracefully. For this she was thankful.

But her kindly nature did not allow her to perceive the workings deep within that malignant brain. A plan had occurred to Buz, and if it proved successful he would have everything he desired. One night, hours before the regular arrival of his shadowy nocturnal caller, another came to the chamber of Buz. There; an agreement that met with the approval of all was consummated.

CHAPTER TEN

THE FOREST OF SOTHOR

In the hours following the river crossing, Dulok had pushed further into the dense foliage. Now, at the height of the afternoon, only the barest traces of sunlight found their way to the floor of the steamy forest. It was as if the light of day chose to shun this foul place, which Dulok had guessed, and Ibdan had confirmed, was the Forest of Sothor. Why had he chosen to come this way? Why not follow the river far south, where a safe crossing into Shadzea could be easily made? Did he really seek a shorter path to the City of Gods, or had an inbred sense of adventure and curiosity surfaced? This fourth Princes' Trial represented the first time he had departed the City of Kings on his own. Surely he had encountered enough danger and excitement in the Desert of Craters to last most men a lifetime. Yet the opportunity was here, the chance to tell all that he had traversed the Forest of Sothor, the forbidden place of the legends, and survived; that the demons they so feared were but shadows from the superstitious minds of those long dead, the ones who chose to fear that which they did not understand.

Dulok's limited experience with the barren, rugged plains of Shadzea could not have prepared him for the wonders he beheld in this new environment. Thick boled trees rose high above him, their leafy boughs disappearing into the high ceiling of dense mist that shrouded the forest. Wide, fanlike fronds of diverse hues offered the illusion of striding through a living rainbow. Sleek vines and creepers snaked their way across the rich loam, as well as around the trunks of the glistening trees. Life seemed to be everywhere around him, and yet Dulok realized that, save for the crunching of foliage beneath the hooves of the horses, the forest was still. No bird sang, no insect chirruped; there were no coughs or roars of predators, no hoofbeats of escaping prey. For the first time some sinister aspect of this wood struck him, and despite the stifling heat and humidity, he pulled his robe tightly around him to ward off an unexpected chill.

Ibdan's steed had long since been released, but still it chose to follow closely behind Dulok's stallion, for once across the Kobur it had lost its homing instinct. They traveled in a direction that the prince judged to be the shortest distance to the City of Gods. The foliage along this route at first appeared even more plentiful and quite lush, but soon it had begun to thin, and Dulok's sensitive nostrils detected the fetid odor of decay. Soon the stench choked the Shadzean, as all about him the forest took on new characteristics. Blackened stumps of trees lay strangled by rotted vines. The once rich soil was soft, foul-smelling mud. The gentle mist that floated overhead swirled uneasily, and Dulok noticed an eerie purplish tinge visible throughout it. The air was definitely more chilled now, and even through the heavy robe Dulok could feel the thin, gelid fingers as they jabbed menacingly at him.

The two horses snorted nervously as the trek through the reeking forest wore on. Their keen senses detected all that Dulok perceived, and more. Unable to see the source of their consternation, they nonetheless knew it was there. Sinuous, reddish creepers snaked their way through the mud at the feet of the steeds, and once the intruders had passed, the bulbous tips of these obscene vines undulated upward, stopping many feet above the earth. The tip then curled, like the head of some unspeakable serpent from the murky depths of the Telliun Ocean. Unseeing sensors located the intruders, and when their position had been fixed the plant began to vibrate. A humming noise ensued, and it permeated the sphere, as if the entire wood was being alerted to this unwanted presence in their midst. No human ears could detect this subtle sound, but the sharp ears of the horses could, and as such their fear was greater than that of the unknowing Dulok.

The foul stench of decay and death became the air that the young prince breathed, and at times he choked, for the density of the effluvium clogged his lungs. The reddish creepers were everywhere now, hanging down from the boughs of blackened trees as well as crawling across the putrid loam. But through these creepers and the low-hanging mist, Dulok espied something that brought him to a halt in the midst of a small clearing. What looked like the crumbling ruins of a long dead city stood before him, the vine-encrusted walls rising to only a few feet above his own height. Whatever civilization this had been, it appeared that its own defense against outside invaders had not been one of its prime interests. Am I mad, thought Dulok, or does the chill of this accursed forest seem to emanate from the direction of these ruins?

The young prince sat high atop his stallion and contemplated the exploration of this dead city. So transfixed were his eyes upon the ruins that he failed to perceive of what was occurring only yards above his head. Indeed, had he even noticed it might not have immediately registered in his brain, so insignificant did it appear. A thin wisp of bluish smoke wended its way amidst the rotted branches of a lofty tree, the boughs of which stretched out into the clearing above Dulok. Slowly, as if with purpose, it snaked downward, until only inches separated it from the prince's thick, unkempt shock of black hair. The horses immediately sensed this new presence. Each snorted nervously, and the more agitated desert pony pawed the ground in fright. Dulok turned to calm the steed, but so quickly did the wisp dart away that even the trained eye of a hunting falcon would not have noticed.

The wisp reappeared high in the trees, but this time three other strands floated gently beside it. Together they retraced the original route downward, again stopping near the intruder's head. The desert pony saw them, and this time its terror was great. It reared high in the air, its eyes ablaze, and bolted back into the forest. Dulok promptly turned, and this time he too saw them. He stared at them incredulously, unable to conceive of what they might be, or what purpose they had. His stallion reared slightly, but he managed to keep it under control.

Now the ethereal strands darted at Dulok's face. They seemed to pass through him as contact was made, but each time a peculiar tingling sensation caused him to jump. He swatted at them viciously, but found nothing substantial. Again and again they swirled about his face, as well as that of the horse. The fine stallion, though unwilling to desert its master, nevertheless was overwhelmed with terror. It reared high in the air, throwing Dulok, who had loosed the reins in order to ward off the wisps, to the decayed earth below. It then bolted into the forest on the trail of its fellow, and disappeared.

Dulok, though slightly stunned, was unhurt by the fall, due to the softness of the loam. He would have risen to his feet and set off in pursuit of the animal, but the clearing, empty only moments before, now swarmed with many dark-robed figures. They climbed atop Dulok, and so numerous were they that he had no time to unsheath his blade. They disarmed him quickly and bound his hands behind his back. He was then hauled to his feet and shoved forward in the direction of the city he had thought to be dead.

"Another outsider," Dulok heard one of them hiss. "*He* will be pleased. They appear to be much concerned, and well they should be."

The speaker received no reply from his fellows, nor was another word spoken the rest of the way. The floating strands that had first caused the misfortunes were nowhere to be seen, and Dulok wondered if his mind had toyed with him. But he recalled the horses, and he knew that they too had seen the phenomenon, or at least sensed it.

One of Dulok's sinister captors walked in front of him, while the rest brought up the rear. He could not study any of their features due to the heavy robes, but he was certain they were not Fashaars. They were taller than most of the Fashaars, though their backs were bent. The accent of the one who had spoken denoted a westerner, and was most unlike the gutteral tones of the desert dwellers. Dulok had no idea who his captors might be, but just their habitation alone in this forest of horrors bode ill for him.

The portal into the city, unseen from a distance due to the foliage that blocked it, had no door or gate. Though wide enough for the legions of some powerful nation to pass through, it appeared that none ever had. Within the city there were few men to be seen along the unpaved streets, and even fewer women. Numerous structures of mud and rocks, many only half built and then abandoned, lined these streets in haphazard fashion. The ubiquitous red creepers had long since found their way into the city, lending an even more spectral appearance.

Along avenues wide enough to accommodate twenty abreast, and through alleys so narrow that one had to turn sideways to pass, the young prince of Shadzea was guided. Once he risked turning his head, but the well-honed end of a longsword forced his eyes forward. This sham of a city, compared to those he had seen in Shadzea, offended his senses, but a morbid fascination allowed him to continue absorbing all that he passed.

A corner was turned, and a structure far larger than any Dulok had seen stood at the end of a wide avenue. Other than its size there was little that could be considered impressive about it. It too had been put together crudely, but unlike the others it appeared to be completed. Only a few of the creepers clung to its sides, although in many other places there were wide patches of dark green moss, which at first glance appeared to be a paint or dye. The opening that afforded ingress, like the main portal to the city, had no door, nor any other

142

obstruction. The leaders of this place surely feared nothing, thought Dulok, or perhaps they were crazed.

Into this building the prince of Shadzea was led. The procession passed between rows of statues, figures of what Dulok dared not even guess. Some bore heads that appeared human, while the remainder of the body was not. Others were the antithesis of this, with grotesque skulls atop bodies of human perfection. There were glistening, shapeless figures carved of obsidian, and caricatures of malformed animals made of pure gold. In the darkened halls of this obscene temple the figures somehow seemed alive, and the disgusted Dulok averted his eyes to the floor, lest his already overtaxed mind toy further with him.

From the center of this building, which was even more spacious than Dulok had thought, came a low, steady hum of voices. To the prince it brought to mind the supplications offered Doj and Bao by the red priests in the great temples, which Dulok had visited in the City of Gods. But what foul deities could consider this place a hall of worship? Dulok shuddered at the thought, but still he would have been curious to discover the answer, no matter how grim. The opportunity was not to be his, however, for his guide turned to the left and entered a dark corridor, and he was obliged to follow.

The short hallway ended in a descending flight of poorly constructed stairs. Some were quite wide, while others were narrow, and with the next step possibly being further along, it would have been a simple matter to miss one and suffer serious injury. Dulok watched his footing well during the descent, and minutes later the steps terminated in a long, narrow corridor, this poorly lighted by a few unevenly spaced torches that hung from oddly shaped sconces on earthen walls. Dulok saw other cowled figures, two of them standing in front of a small wooden door. A door! It was the first that Dulok had seen since entering this city. But then, he reasoned, what would one expect to find in a prison?

The guards nodded grimly at Dulok's captors, but still no words were exchanged. One of the former opened the door, and Dulok was forced to stoop in order to pass through. The lead captor gave him a vicious shove with his foot, and the prince was catapulted headlong into the Stygian cell. Before he could regain his feet the door was slammed shut, and the outside bolt dropped into place. Dulok's freedom, regained from the mines of the Fashaars, had indeed been short-lived.

Dulok returned to the door and attempted to peer out into the dark corridor, but the narrow crack in the door offered him little to see. He decided to traverse the black cell in an effort to learn of its size, as well as to see if any other means of egress were at hand. Slowly, deliberately, he paced along the perimeter of the cell, his left foot purposely scraping the wall. He had counted ten paces from the door when he ran into a wall. He turned left and continued. The wall appeared to curve slightly, but it remained solid. After twenty-seven paces Dulok reached the back wall, and as he turned to continue his futile exploration, he realized that his hopes were ebbing.

"I pray you do not trample me, friend!" The voice came from in front of him, and the startled prince froze.

"Who—who is there?" he asked warily.

"Another unfortunate prisoner, much as yourself," the voice answered. It was a strong voice, and had spirit. "Come, recline on the floor by me and I will tell you all you wish to know about this cell, for I have paced its

144

every inch a hundred times."

Dulok moved closer and stared in the direction of the voice, and as his eyes grew more accustomed to the darkness he discerned the outline of a strapping young man. Apparently the fellow had not been here for a considerable length of time, or his body would have withered.

"Here, sit by me so that I might see you better," said the cheerful voice. "My eyes are well accustomed to this accursed blackness, and—by the gods, Dulok! It is Dulok! My prince, what ill fortune brings you to this place?"

"Who are you?" asked the surprised Shadzean. "How would one here know of me?"

"I am Turnivo, my prince, son of Ayo, the red priest. You would not know me, but surely all in Shadzea know of you. I saw you once when, with my father, I visited the City of Kings."

"So you are Turnivo, son of Ayo, are you?" said Dulok, and Turnivo noted the slightest hint of a smile on the prince's face. "How strange indeed are the fates, that they should throw us together like this in such a foul place."

"You appear to know of me," said the amazed young man. "But how can this be? I am an obscure son of a priest, and you—"

"I *know* who you are, Turnivo," Dulok stated emphatically.

"You—you *know?*" Turnivo appeared not to believe what he had heard. "But this is impossible! How could you have found out?"

"There are more important things worthy of discussion at present," said Dulok vaguely.

"But if you know, then would you not wish to kill me?" Turnivo asked.

"Do you have any desire to destroy me?" Dulok countered.

"Of course not, but—"

"Then I have your word on it, as you have mine." Dulok's statement was final. "I would have eventually sought you out anyway. Now, enough of this! Tell me, in what foul dungeon are we kept prisoner?"

"You mean you do not know?" Turnivo was further amazed.

"I would not have asked otherwise," the impatient Dulok snapped. "I know that I entered the northern forest from the east. That is all."

"The Forest of Sothor, my prince," whispered Turnivo, almost in awe. "This is the Forest of Sothor, and we rot in the dungeons below the City of Necromancy! Surely one such as yourself has been reared in the history of your own people, and know of this!"

"I have listened to the tales since childhood, but I have considered them nothing more than old legends. Now you tell me that they are true?"

"The red priests of Doj and Bao have always known this, and in the face of much skepticism from past Survivors they have quietly seen to it that Shadzea has always been protected from the foul curse that Sothor placed on Dain, the Pious One, so long ago. Yes, my prince, the legends are indeed true."

"But what of this Sothor?" the stunned Dulok asked. "Does he exist? And what of you, Turnivo? What brings you here from the City of Gods?"

"Sothor is no myth, my prince, for already I have set

146

eyes upon his vile countenance, and have witnessed the perpetration of unspeakable acts. I journeyed here to see if what all in the City of Gods feared was true. I learned what I came for, and had it not been for my foolish curiosity I might have escaped the forest undetected."

"And what did you learn here, at the risk of your life?" Dulok asked.

"I departed immediately after the theft of the Stone of Bao," Turnivo related. "The red priests believe that Sothor knows, whether by earthly means or—or otherwise, of all occurrences that might be of interest to him. I wished to learn if this accursed son of Esh knew of the theft, or if—the gods help us—he himself was the perpetrator. Here I discovered that the theft of the stone was known to him, but he himself did not assign the robbers. This was fortunate, but it only meant a delay. He knew that the stone was carried far into the inaccessible Desert of Craters by the Fashaars, and that few ever return from that inferno. He began the Summoning, to which I bore witness one dreaded night. Every night now he tries, and it is only a matter of time before he can convince *Them!*"

"Your words are strange to me, Turnivo," said the confused Dulok. "What is this Summoning? Who are those that Sothor must convince? And what is it he must convince them of?"

"The Summoning is—" Turnivo paused, and shuddered. "I find it difficult to relate, so horrid was it to witness. It is the calling forth of the Dark Ones from the deepest, most foul pits of Esh. You recall the prophecy of Sothor, given to Dain before the sorcerer was expelled from our land?"

"That the demons of Esh will crawl up and overrun the

147

land, until no human is left," Dulok offered. "All have heard of this."

"The Summoning is the act that precedes the final destruction," Turnivo went on. "For many nights following the theft of the stone Sothor attempted a Summoning, until finally a singular demon crawled forth in answer to the call. Two nights later a second appeared, and two nights after that a third. Every second night now the number increases. On the night that I saw them there were half a score. He has convinced some, and through them he will convince all. Once this is done it will be over, for none shall fear to crawl up and walk the earth." Turnivo again shuddered, this time almost convulsively.

"But still you have not told me! What is it that the Dark Ones must be convinced of?"

"The Stone of Bao is the singular power that keeps these horrors in their pits of slime. Its presence once drove Sothor out of the land, and knowledge of its existence in the City of Gods has stayed his hand these many years. No one, not even the red priests, fully understand its power. Some say that the gods themselves fashioned the jewel, while others believe that it is a piece that had broken off an even larger stone, one which fell from the clouds near the dawn of time. Whatever the case it is gone now, and when Sothor convinces the Dark Ones that they can walk the land with impunity, it will spell our doom. Once all have risen the power of the stone shall be negated, even were it recovered. This latter fact is one that I learned during my sojourn here, a fact not even known by the red priests."

Dulok appeared thoughtful for a moment, before stating: "Is that all?"

"*Is that all?*" Turnivo snapped. "Many pardons, my

prince, but are you a fool to say such a thing?"

Dulok laughed softly. "I followed those who took the stone into the Desert of Craters, journeying many leagues to the north before my search came to an end. I need not relate all that transpired, but, suffice it to say, the stone is safe. You see, Turnivo, I have the Stone of Bao with me!"

Turnivo stared incredulously at Dulok. "Surely you toy with me, my prince!" he scowled. "Would that such a thing be true!"

"Were my hands not tied I would be pleased to show you," stated Dulok, and his frankness convinced the doubtful young man. "The acolytes did a poor job of searching me, or they would have been in for quite a shock."

"I—I cannot believe this!" said Turnivo joyously. "You are more than a prince, Dulok; perhaps even more than a man. Surely you are destined to become the—"

"Let that be!" Dulok ordered. "It appears that we have more important things to do. But first we must flee this foul hole."

"Then allow me to speak, my prince, for in my months of internment I have devised many plans, most of which require another to assist me. Now, here is what we must do . . ."

Bori found the note tacked to his door, and he gasped with horror as he read it. In the hope that it was the work of some prankster he rushed to his daughter's chamber, only to find it vacant. He explored the garden, her favorite spot, but this too was empty. With a sinking heart he realized that the note bore no idle threats. He hurried with it to the chamber of Ornon, and from Bori's distraught look the king knew that something was wrong. He postponed his daily affairs and had his chamber emptied of all, save his trusted old counselor.

"Your troubled look foretells bad news, my friend," Ornon stated. "What is wrong?"

"My king, forgive the intrusion," Bori pleaded, "but I found this note. It is from Blotono. He has kidnapped Sallia, and he demands great riches for her return!"

"Blotono! The devil!" Ornon roared. "But how could he have accomplished such a deed, and right under our noses? No matter. I have desired to crush him for years. I will gather the forces of Shadzea, and we will march to the City of Rogues!"

"My pardons, Sire," Bori interrupted. "It states here in the note that any display of force will instantly result in her death. I fear that he will not hesitate to carry this out."

"Of course you are right," Ornon replied pensively. "Something else will have to be done. But what?"

Buz and his mentor had entered Ornon's chamber only moments before on some pretext of business, and could not help but overhear the conversation. Buz rushed to the side of Bori, concern masking his face.

"Tell me that what I just heard was not true!" the worried Buz snapped. "My dear Sallia could not have been abducted!"

"It is true!" said Ornon. "Even now we discuss how we might free her. Blotono has demanded—"

"Blotono! The accursed pirate!" Buz roared. "By the gods, I swear that this crime will not go unpunished! Hear me, Sire, and you, Bori, the father of my beloved: I will journey alone to the City of Rogues, by way of the Terven Marshes, and I will free Sallia. She shall be safely

150

returned to the City of Kings, along with the head of Blotono, which shall be hung in the square for all to see. This, my king, I propose as my fourth Princes' Trial!"

"I will surely sanction such an act!" announced the proud king. "Where is my scribe? Buz's choice must be duly noted. Prepare yourself, so that you might leave in the morning. May the gods go with you!"

On the following morning the first son departed the City of Kings, and the wishes of all went along with him. But there was one who found much uncertainty in all that had transpired since the previous day. Less than an hour after the departure of Buz he too rode forth from the City of Kings, but there were none to see him off. He pointed his horse toward the southwest, in the direction of the Terven Marshes, and after much hard riding he was able to pick up the trail he sought.

CHAPTER ELEVEN

THE SUMMONING OF THE DARK ONES

The door creaked open slowly, for the time had come to provide the prisoners with whatever meager fare was necessary to sustain their worthless lives, until their fate could be determined. First a torch was thrust in and waved menacingly about, in case a prisoner chose to stand too near the door. After that the food was shoved in, and the door would have been slammed shut. But before they could complete their task, the acolytes heard a sound coming from the back of the cell, and they listened. It was a deep, pitiful moaning, as if someone was in great pain.

"Please! This fellow you brought in is quite ill, and I fear he will die!" shouted a voice from the same direction. "Hurry, for he needs help!"

The acolytes entered cautiously, closing the door behind them. They were uncertain what to do, for they lacked guidance. But they knew that Sothor desired to keep his prisoners alive, and as such they thought it would be wise to see what was wrong. The one with the torch strode across the cell, the other, he assumed, close at his heels. But when he reached the back wall he found no wretched, bound prisoners, but a grimly smiling Turnivo. The guard quickly wheeled about, but instead of his fellow he saw another tall young man, a mask of determination on his face. The crumpled remains of the other lay in the center of the cell. Before he could cry out he felt steellike fingers tighten about his throat. It took only seconds for Turnivo to dispose of him.

The pair had sat back to back for many frustrating hours before finally managing, with numbed fingers, to loosen each other's ties. The rest was but a simple matter, using Turnivo's plan, and the two were pleased at the result.

"Quickly, my prince," Turnivo ordered. "Let us don their robes and depart, before the others decide to look in."

Dulok exchanged garments with one of the dead acolytes, while Turnivo followed suit. The mere touch of the fouled cloth repulsed both of them, but they knew that it would be their only way out. They then propped the guards up on the back wall, lest anyone notice their crumpled bodies on the floor. They approached the cell door and opened it slowly. The corridor guards tensed as it creaked open, but they relaxed when they saw their fellows emerge.

"What ails the prisoner?" one of them inquired.

"The Shadzean dog only thinks himself ill," Dulok rasped. "He will pray for death before Sothor is finished with him."

All laughed heartily, and the cell door was bolted shut. No others would appear to feed the prisoners until the next day, and the two hoped that this would allow them sufficient time to carry out their plan. They shuffled slowly to the uneven stairway and ascended it. Once on the upper level they found their way to the corridor of statues. Others strode along this path, and all appeared to be exiting the temple.

"Hurry, hurry!" shouted one of the acolytes to no one in particular. "It grows dark, and soon it will be time. Hurry!"

Indeed, it was much darker outside, although the unending pall that surrounded the city surely had much to do with this. But even so night would soon fall, and in the dark hours, according to Turnivo, the Summoning would begin. The two Shadzeans broke away from the others who walked near them, and in the darkness they found the sanctuary of a half-built hovel.

"Your plan has worked well so far, my friend," Dulok offered.

"But there is so much more to do," replied Turnivo worriedly. "May the gods see us through the completion of our night's work."

"Turnivo, I really don't know what to do with the stone," Dulok admitted. "Allow me to turn it over to you, so that the will of Bao might properly be carried out."

Dulok dug deeply into his robes, and from the safety of his tattered breechcloth he removed the amulet and handed it to the astonished Turnivo. The young man clutched it to his bosom like some great object of love. He then turned it over in his hands and examined it.

"Never did I believe I would see it again," he stated. "It will surely be put to the test this night."

"But what does it do?" the puzzled Dulok asked. "How can it be made to work?"

"From light and heat does it draw its strength!"

154

Turnivo answered emphatically. "There will be much of this, for on this night the fiery aura of Sothor joins with the flames of Esh. Fear not, my prince, for I know we won't fail!"

Dulok yielded to the leadership of this young man, who seemed possessed with the strength and knowledge, as well as the desire, to save his world. They rose to their feet, and after concealing the amulet in his robes, Turnivo led Dulok out of the City of Necromancy through another unprotected portal, one which Dulok guessed was located on the west wall. Turnivo had told Dulok of a field, some miles from the city, where Sothor gathered his minions for the Summoning. This was surely desecrated ground, and who would have doubted that Sothor himself had been spawned from this place? From the many torches that moved in a like direction, Dulok was certain that his companion knew where he was headed.

The light from the flickering torches of the acolytes produced eerie shadows in the dark, foreboding forest. The numerous creepers seemed to come alive all about them, and to Dulok it was as if the forest itself was aware of the unholy activities that would pervade it that night.

In the distance, Dulok suddenly noted a strange luminescence. He looked questioningly at Turnivo, who nodded grimly. The place of the Summoning was near, and the already chilled air of the forest began to bite deeper and deeper into the flesh of the Shadzeans. Those acolytes that they could see nearby appeared not to notice the cold, for this was their environment, the essence of their evil existence; it was what they knew.

The place of the Summoning was in the center of a vast, natural amphitheater, carved near the dawn of time perhaps, from black shale. The diameter of the floor was at least a hundred yards. From their position near the top, Dulok and Turnivo could see the torches of hundreds, no, thousands of acolytes, far more than Dulok could have imagined existed here. But it was not their torches that had sent forth the glow noticed by him further back in the forest. The very floor of the amphitheater was aglow, emitting a light that throbbed repeatedly as it varied in intensity. At times it was so bright that Dulok was forced to shield his eyes. What foul place was this? he thought, but he feared that he knew the answer all too well.

The procession through the forest was over, and all were now gathered in the rock-bound arena. The earth itself seemed to sense that all was in readiness, for it flared brilliantly, and the radiance did not abate. A low murmur echoed throughout the amphitheater from the hushed conversations of the acolytes, whose own level of excitement had begun to rise in anticipation of subsequent events.

An icy wind suddenly permeated the arena, and the torches of the acolytes flickered wildly, though none were extinguished. So forceful was this breeze that Dulok found it difficult to maintain his footing, and had he not spread his feet he would surely have toppled forward. He pulled his robe tightly around him to ward off the cold, and as he stood there shivering he encountered a new and terrible sensation. In the midst of the biting cold he was struck by a searing gust of air. For only an instant did he feel this, as if some unseen force had passed through him. He gazed at Turnivo, and he knew that this son of priests had sensed it also. Dulok wished to turn and flee this godless place, for an unholy terror had begun to well up inside him, but he knew that he could not. A stern look from Turnivo warned him that this sham must be maintained at all cost.

The radiance from the arena floor abated drastically, and all saw that Sothor was there. That was all; he was not there, and then he was. It seemed as though he had been there all along, and none, save the Shadzeans, exhibited amazement. The murmur from their throats ceased however, and an evil silence now strangled the air about them, as if denoting a prelude to some unspeakable, demented drama.

The shadowy figure that stood alone on the floor of the amphitheater appeared to be of giant proportions to Dulok, for such was the illusion of terror. In truth the sorcerer, though tall, was of a similar height as the prince himself. He was thin, and aged, but no more so than the day he had faced Dain and had been driven from Shadzea, hundreds of years ago. His wizened face was the quintessence of evil, with cruel, piercing eyes and a twisted mouth. When he walked he appeared to limp, for such was the mark of Dain on the sorcerer, one that he would carry to his death, and beyond.

"Acolytes of Sothor, join me, so that the Summoning might begin!" screamed the sorcerer in a voice that resounded through the arena.

The black-robed figures walked slowly down toward their mentor, as if they were mesmerized. Some quitted the shale bleachers for the glowing floor, but even these souls remained along the outer perimeter. Dulok and Turnivo also moved closer, but they stayed as far back as possible without being conspicuous. The sorcerer, satisfied with the positioning of his minions, continued:

"Hear me, young ones, and know what I say!" he

shrieked. "Zyzzaz has sent me a sign, a sign that the Dark Ones waver! Even Uuoulo confirms this, and feels that the time is near. Do you hear me, my children? *The time nears!* Let the Summoning commence!"

The acolytes, as one, dropped to their knees, and the Shadzeans followed suit. They then began to chant, and the melding of many voices rose in the chill night as a singular voice, well modulated and terrible.

"*Astastu Esh! Astastu Esh!*" The chant was repeated over and over. "*Astastu Esh! Astastu Esh! Astastu Esh!*" Ten, fifty, a hundred times, until their bodies quivered with ecstasy. The earth radiated with new fire, which was reflected in the gleaming, insane eyes of Sothor. He stood with his hands outstretched to the darkness above. With a swift motion he dropped them, and the chanting ceased.

"*Astastu Esh! Astastu Esh!*" the sorcerer intoned. "*Vyvixa Ozru Nofyrdix Astastu Esh! Cuvatik Izxtu Yaqig Astastu Esh!*"

"*Astastu Esh! Astastu Esh!*" the acolytes repeated. "*Vyvixa Ozru Nofyrdix Astastu Esh! Cuvatik Izxtu Yaqig Astastu Esh!*"

Dulok shuddered from the mere implications of the strange, chilling language. Turnivo nodded knowledgeably to himself, for all in the City of Gods recognized the words that marked the foul tongue of the Dark Ones. He did not know what the words meant, but he knew that they portended only evil.

"*Astastu Esh! Astastu Esh!*" Sothor continued. "*Cuvatik Zyzzaz! Cuvatik Uuoulo! Cuvatik Zyzzaz! Cuvatik Uuoulo!*"

"*Cuvatik Zyzzaz! Cuvatik Uuoulo!*" screamed the acolytes.

"*Cuvatik Yvexxis! Cuvatik Tytuokm!*" chanted Sothor.

"*Astastu Esh! Astastu Esh!*" the acolytes answered. "*Cuvatik Zyzzaz! Cuvatik Uuoulo! Cuvatik Yvexxis! Cuvatik Tytuokm!*"

"*Astastu Esh! Astastu Esh!*" The frenzied sorcerer now screamed his words. "*Vyvixa Ozru Nofyrdix Astastu Esh! Cuvatik Zyzzaz!*"

"*Cuvatik Zyzzaz! Cuvatik Zyzzaz!*" countered his minions. "*Astastu Esh!*"

The radiating earth now rumbled, and in front of the disbelieving eyes of Dulok a tiny rift opened in the center of the amphitheater. It widened slowly as the rumbling continued, until a yawning chasm was visible. Still the vibrations persisted, while Sothor and his followers drew closer around the crack.

"*Astastu Esh! Astastu Esh!*" screamed Sothor. "*Cuvatik Zyzzaz! Cuvatik Zyzzaz!*" His minions repeated the words.

From the depths of this Stygian hole rose a force, and all who were there, including the Shadzeans, became aware of its presence as it drew nearer. Over the edge of the chasm something appeared, and it took hold of the edge, as if to pull itself up. To Dulok it seemed formless, a putrid blob that continually altered it contours. But presently it evolved into a more recognizable shape, that of a deformed hand!

Cuvatik Zyzzaz! Cuvatik Zyzzaz!" all shouted, as if to urge the thing on. Slowly it pulled itself over the edge of the gaping hole, and the sickened Dulok witnessed a bulbous mass of colorless slime, this exuding foul droppings in its wake as it undulated clumsily away from the vile pit that spewed it forth. At times it would alter its shape, and for brief instances the prince could identify its outlines as that of—the gods prevent it—a human being!

159

"Cuvatik Uuoulo! Cuvatik Yvexxis! Cuvatik Tytuokm!" screamed the minions, now all but ignoring this abomination in their midst. *"Astastu Esh! Astastu Esh!"*

Slowly, tantalizingly, the chasm spewed forth monstrosities that could not have been conceived in the blackest depths of the most depraved mind. The statues in the temple of the City of Necromancy came to Dulok's mind, and he now knew where the models for such unspeakable art work had been born. A roaring creature, more than twice the size of a man, emerged. Its hairy, malformed face displayed vicious fangs, while atop its outsized head sat two tiny antlers. Its glistening ebony body, however, was the essence of human perfection. Close behind it crawled another creature of slime, similar to the first but even larger. A pulsating red light emanated from it, and one could see, within the creature, the black, viscous fluid that was its life blood.

"Cuvatik Tytuokm! Cuvatik Tytuokm!" the minions howled, while the horrors crawled among them. *"Cuvatik Tytuokm! Cuvatik Tytuokm!"*

Dulok stared incredulously at the crazed scene, and a great sickness welled up within his stomach. He fought the urge to gag, and he prayed that somehow this would soon end. He had not noticed Turnivo, who had started to move forward on his own, but now returned to see that Dulok was by his side. He put his hand on the prince's shoulder, and he smiled grimly.

"It is time," he stated.

Something else had begun to emerge, something huge and unspeakable. Sothor and the acolytes chanted ecstatically, and the horrors that had already joined them shared in their rapture. But none among them were prepared for what was to happen next, for a loud voice pierced even the frenzied din of the amphitheater and brought all to momentary silence.

"Sothor, hear me, for this foul madness will cease!" shouted the voice, and all stared in the direction from which it came. There they saw two whom they had thought of their own number, but with their hoods turned down none could recognize them.

"What cursed fools dare interfere with the Summoning?" the sorcerer shrieked. "Don't you know what you are doing?"

"I am Turnivo, your prisoner these recent months, and this is Dulok, son of Ornon. Know this, vile one, before your revelry ceases!"

"Do you hear that, my children, and you, Dark Ones? The son of a priest brings with him the son of a king! We have such noble witnesses to the beginning of the end for their people. And you, Dulok, a descendant of Dain. A sweet way for my vengeance to begin, would you not agree?" The acolytes laughed wickedly, while the abominations hissed and moaned in mockery of the intruders.

"Look here, foul ones, and know that your time has come!" From within his robes Turnivo drew forth the Stone of Bao and held it high above his head. Those below saw the jewel flicker in the dazzling light, and they realized that the misdeeds of their lifetimes were about to be expunged.

"But this cannot be!" shrieked Sothor insanely as the Shadzeans descended deeper into the arena. "The Stone of Bao was lost forever in the Desert of Craters! The Dark Ones, they believed me, and they came—!"

"See the stone, Dark Ones," Turnivo shouted, "and know that it is in your midst! Let it force you back into the putrid pits that bred you, there to remain until time itself is done! Take with you this creature who called you forth with falsehoods, so that he would trouble us no more!"

Some of the acolytes were scurrying up the sides of the amphitheater, to disappear into the gloom of the forest. Others, more frenzied than their fellows, hurled themselves screaming into the black pit to an unknown fate below. The Stone of Bao began to pulsate in Turnivo's hands, and from its core a beam of bluish light poured forth into the first of the shapeless horrors. A scream emanated from the thing, though no orifice was visible. It began to liquify, and slowly it seeped toward the hole and poured downward into the bottomless chasm. The ebony horror with the horned skull roared viciously and leaped into the hole to avoid the beam, but the thin light found the third of them. This travesty screamed as it too began to dissolve, but before it could disappear entirely over the edge it wrapped a molten tentacle around the cringing Sothor. The sorcerer shrieked as the Dark One dragged him slowly downward.

"*No! No! Do not take me back!*" he cried. "*I did not mean to fail! How could I know they would find it? How could I know? Please! I wish to stay! Don't—take—me— back—!*"

Only his hand remained outside the chasm, and his long fingernails dug frantically into the hard earth. But this was to no avail, and the two Shadzeans could hear his screams diminish as he made the final descent. Turnivo then pointed the beam into the gaping hole, and again the earth shook. Turnivo saw the crack slowly close, and he was satisfied. He began to pocket the amulet, when he heard Dulok shout.

"Turnivo, look! The forest is in flames! The acolytes must have scattered torches in their haste to flee! We must leave here!"

"The destruction of this forest is in far greater hands than the remains of Sothor's minions," Turnivo replied. "But you are right; we must depart!"

They quitted the amphitheater and raced into the forest, while the flames rose high around them. They hastened southward, for Turnivo was familiar with the forest, even at night. Many frightened acolytes were encountered, and these ragged creatures begged them for aid, but they were shoved aside.

They were passing through a clearing when two huge shapes bore down on them. At first Dulok thought that the madness of the night had not as yet ended, but it took him only a moment to recognize his fine stallion and the desert pony. Surely the gods were with them, he thought. He called to his animal, and quickly calmed the beast. Turnivo commandeered the other steed, and together the two young Shadzeans rode swiftly to the south, the rapidly spreading flames only yards behind them.

Two young men stood along the perimeter of the forest and watched the smoke curl high in the air. The sun had just peered over the horizon, and it was likely that this smoke would be visible for miles. But who was there to see it, and who would know what it portended even if they did? Only this pair knew, and soon they would share the knowledge with all their people.

Dulok looked at Turnivo and smiled. "It is over," he stated simply.

"Yes, it is over, my prince," Turnivo replied. "Now we may go home."

"The horses are fatigued, as I'm sure we both are," said Dulok. "Let us rest here for the time being. Besides, my friend, there is much for us to talk about."

CHAPTER TWELVE

TRIUMPH AND TRAGEDY

The long journey from the edge of the forest to the City of Gods across the barren, sparsely populated provinces of Shadzea offered little adventure to the determined pair who traversed the many tedious miles. True, there was always the occasional brigand, and once they were even cornered by a well organized band; but it would have taken quite a bit more to deter these two from their goal. They had fought and conquered the worst horrors of Esh, and no one would have denied them their feeling of invincibility.

At the time that Dulok and Turnivo made their way across the wastelands of Shadzea, another grim rider quietly stole through the gates of the City of Kings. His entry went unchallenged, for all recognized Qual, mentor to one of the Twenty. It was Qual who had followed Buz from the city, for the wise mentor had doubted the integrity of Buz's quest from the first. There was nothing he could offer anyone as proof, so he had decided to take the matter into his own hands. His interest in the advancement of his princely charge was secondary to his concern over the safety of Sallia, and he knew that Dulok's feelings would be no different. Whether Dulok were alive or dead, Qual still felt that this responsibility was his.

Qual had followed Buz for many miles, and initially it appeared that the first son was sincere in his words, for he rode straight toward the Terven Marshes, the quickest, albeit the most deadly path to the City of Rogues. But only hours after departing the city Buz made rendezvous with a large wagon, the occupants of which were three questionable ruffians. They greeted Buz cheerfully, as though they were expecting him, and the prince reciprocated in kind. He then joined these villains in the comfortable, well provisioned cart, his steed being tied to the rear. The party changed direction and set out toward the northwest. From his vantage point the astonished Qual watched the wagon disappear over a ridge, and he urged his own mount in a like direction.

Many hours later, the mentor realized that Buz had no intention of resuming his course through the Terven Marshes, as he had sworn. Simple deduction told him that this present course would skirt the marshes and deposit Buz on the shore of the Telliun Ocean, many miles north of the City of Rogues. Here he would most likely commandeer a vessel and sail to the city. While far safer, it was also a time consuming journey, and would greatly delay the rescue of Sallia.

As he rode back to the City of Kings, Qual had considered making known the activities of Buz to Ornon and the council, an act that surely would have destroyed the ambitions of the prince. Just the fact alone that he had accepted help from others in his quest would have been sufficient. But he thought of Dulok, the youth he had raised and cared for, the man he respected. That Dulok would not have it this way Qual was certain, and until he was convinced that the prince was dead he would maintain his silence.

There were few within the walls of the City of Kings that Qual trusted, but he did not doubt the loyalty of one small boy. This youth had attached himself to Dulok some years ago, and had become his page. Dulok's kindness to him had won the lad's respect, and love, and there was nothing he would not do for the prince. He dispatched the youth, whose name was Tirri, to the City of Gods with a message for Dulok. He gave the boy the name of a discreet friend, and advised him to stay within the confines of this friend's home until the prince's long awaited arrival became, the gods willing, a reality.

A great fanfare preceded Dulok and Turnivo into the City of Gods, for the outlying villages had already seen the two, and the word spread quickly. Turnivo had long since returned the Stone of Bao to its rightful savior, and he was quick to tell all that the prince's mission had been successful. Dulok was much embarrassed by the excess adulation directed at him, but Turnivo grinned broadly, for he knew that the unbounded joy of the people was well warranted.

Under the gleaming eyes of the red priests, Dulok returned the amulet to its rightful place in the temple. He and Turnivo then advised the head priest of the fate of Sothor, and his expulsion from their midst for all time. The priest was elated, and the word spread among the populace like sagefire. The normally staid citizenry of this holy city celebrated in the streets, such was their joy, and the names of Dulok and Turnivo were on the lips of all. That a prince should accomplish such a feat was most worthy; but such valor from the son of a priest, one of their own? Much pride was shared that day.

Despite the crowds that converged in an effort to merely touch them, Turnivo managed a joyful reunion with Ayo. Turnivo presented Dulok to his father, and the two clasped hands warmly. With additional effort they pushed their way through the throng, until for a moment they found quiet.

"It is a joy to see you again, my son," Ayo beamed proudly.

"And you, Father," Turnivo replied hurriedly. "But listen, for there is something I must tell you. Dulok knows!"

"He—*knows?*" Ayo could not believe what he had heard. "Then we must talk, and soon!"

But the crowd again discovered them, and for hours no further solitude could be found. This was a great day for Shadzea, and none were about to be cheated of their share. Turnivo and Dulok were hoisted from shoulder to shoulder for all to see and laud. Not until nearly sundown, when the head priest struck the ceremonial gong and ordered the temple cleared, did the revelry cease. Turnivo and Dulok, accompanied by the priest's blessings, were led to Ayo's home for much needed rest and refreshment.

The home shared by Ayo and Turnivo, a short distance from the Temple of Bao, was neat and orderly. To Dulok, who had never known such a home, it radiated warmth and affection. He visualized a youthful, mischievous Turnivo laughing, fleeing the grasp of the raging Ayo, on whom he had just played a prank. But the twinkle in the father's eyes told of minimal punishment, and the lad would always allow himself to be captured. He would squeal with delight as the father lifted him high in the air and gently reproached him. Such were the games played by himself and another so long ago, games that were so violently interrupted by the cruel realities of the world into which he had been born. He shook the images from his head and concentrated on the sumptuous feast that had been laid before him by his host.

Ayo, in spite of his intense curiosity regarding what his son had told him in the temple, chose to wait patiently and allow the famished travelers to refresh themselves. Once done the conversation began, and it went uninterrupted for hours. Turnivo occasionally strode outside to assure himself that unwanted ears did not linger nearby, for the bulk of the talk was between Ayo and Dulok. These two, strangers until that day, established a trust in each other that might have taken years with men of less sincerity.

As the sharing of long pent-up secrets reached an end, Turnivo, who sat near the door, became aware of a slight scraping noise just outside. The others had not heard it. Slowly, silently, he rose to his feet and grasped the door handle. With a quick motion he pulled the door inward, and the individual whose ear had been pressed up against it stumbled into the room. Turnivo would have leaped upon the spy, but he noticed his diminutive size.

"Tirri! It is Tirri!" Dulok had recognized the lad, and he smiled broadly. "But why are you here?"

"My prince!" the boy responded happily. "The gods have been good, for they have returned you safely! Since earlier today, when I learned that you had come back, I have tried to reach you, but always the crowds were too heavy. I did not know where you had been taken after dark, and have been searching the streets for hours."

"Does Qual know that you are here?"

"It was Qual who sent me to await you, my prince. I arrived only yesterday morning."

"But why, lad?" Tirri looked suspiciously at Ayo and Turnivo. "They are friends, and you may speak freely in their presence," Dulok assured him.

"Qual has prayed for your life since your departure, my prince," the boy told him, "but not as much as he has in the past few days. He felt that you would want to be advised of what has transpired immediately upon your arrival, if indeed you still lived. He sent me with a message for you."

"Quickly!" Dulok snapped. "Let me see it."

Tirri handed Dulok the sealed note, and all watched his expression alter to one of grave concern and bitterness as he read its words:

Sallia abducted by Blotono, and taken to City of Rogues. Buz in pursuit of her as his Trial of Death, but suspect duplicity on his part. You are needed immediately, for her safety is foremost.

Qual

"You appear troubled, my friend," said Turnivo. "The news is bad?"

Dulok handed the note to Turnivo, who shared its contents with his father. The disturbed Ayo then destroyed the note, as he knew Dulok would wish. He walked to the troubled youth and placed his hand gently on his shoulder.

"And so it grows more difficult each day, my prince," he offered soothingly. "One would have thought your

170

quest nearly at an end. Is there anything we can do?"

"There is, Ayo," Dulok replied. "Gather me food and water, for I must depart tonight. Nothing has changed, of this I assure you. Be in the courtyard on the day of the Reckoning, the two of you. This is all I ask."

"I will come with you!" Turnivo insisted. "With two swords—!"

"You will remain here until the appointed time," Dulok ordered. "If the gods will it that I do not return, you know what must be done. Now, let us speak no more, for I must leave!"

Tirri left to fetch his own steed, and by the time he returned to the home of Ayo he found his master ready. There was little more to be said between Dulok and his hosts, so with a hasty clasping of hands the prince mounted his fine stallion and departed, his young page close at his heels. Ayo and Turnivo watched them turn the corner and disappear down the avenue that would lead them to the main gate. Turnivo shrugged his shoulders and sadly reentered his home, but Ayo knew that immediate sleep would be impossible. He returned to the temples, where he alternately implored Doj and Bao to see the young prince safely to the day of the Reckoning.

Dulok and Tirri rode all through the night, and all the next day, stopping only occasionally for brief periods of rest. The stamina and exuberance of his young squire did not amaze Dulok, for the boy had always shown promise of greater things to come, and now, put to the test, he responded with fervor. People from small villages lined the rugged road between the two cities to catch a glimpse of the prince, for his exploits had already preceded him. He paid them little heed, for in his mind two words were

171

repeated over and over: *Sallia abducted!* What sinister motives underlined such a craven act? Why would Blotono, who had always shunned the City of Kings, suddenly appear? And how convenient for Buz, who had lingered in the palace those long months, to be presented with this opportunity of so worthy a Princes' Trial. Dulok had read much in Qual's few words, and already he was beginning to see his dreams of vengeance, a fitting vengeance that had been pent up within him these many years, fall apart.

The outlying villages began to thin, and the main road became even more rugged. For two more days of difficult travel there were few villages to be seen; but eventually the outskirts of the City of Kings was reached, and the adulation of the hero resumed in earnest. Dulok practically fought his way into his home city, and he was concerned lest Tirri be crushed in the onslaught. Shadzean guards finally maintained some semblance of order, and the young prince was able to ride to the palace unimpeded, amidst the waves and cheers of the citizenry.

In the throne room of the palace sat the king, surrounded by his council, the remaining mentors, and Korb, who had recently returned in triumph with the zkreel he had destroyed in the Telliun Ocean. He bore many scars, but otherwise appeared in good health. There was no sign of Esaaz, nor would any ever see him again in this life, for even at that moment his bleached bones ornamented the lair of an azkor, the beast he would have killed. The Forest of Sothor had worked its horrors on his brain, and by the time he had reached the hills that house these beasts the damage had been done. He was defenseless before the white-furred engine of death.

Dulok offered curt acknowledgement to Korb and to the council, but for many moments he gazed upon Qual, his mentor, who grimly returned the stare. He then turned toward Ornon, and bowed formally.

"Sire," Dulok recited, "I have returned from my fourth and final Princes' Trial, and I claim it to be successful!"

"Your accomplishments precede you, Dulok," said the king. "Nearly all of Shadzea is aware of what you have done. As for official proof, I have here a scroll that I received only days before from the head priest via messenger hawk, advising me that the Stone of Bao now resides in its proper place. But your additional exploits amaze and gratify me even more. I gladly accept your claim, my son, and I am proud to welcome you back."

All surrounded the young prince to offer their congratulations, all save Korb, his mentor, and Lonz. Buz's mentor scowled at this unforeseen circumstance, for none had expected Dulok to return alive, no less in such glory. The task would be even more difficult now, he thought, but it would still be carried through, of this he was certain.

Dulok accepted the kind words of his welcomers vaguely, for at the moment one thought dominated his mind. But in spite of this, he found an instant to ponder on the genuine kindliness of Ornon toward him. In place of the past formalities, the king had reflected pride in the accomplishments of his twentieth son. Dulok felt that Ornon, for the first time, saw in him a son capable of becoming the fifteenth Survivor, a worthy successor to Shadzea's throne. Perhaps a different relationship—

No! Again the scene repeated itself in his mind, as it had done thousands of times previously. He saw Ornon thrust the blade into the helpless Daynea's heart, and he saw the cold, unfeeling expression as he handed the dripping weapon to a guard and exited the scullery. Surely his misdeed had been forgotten by him the very next day. But there was one who did not forget, who would *never* forget. He knew that the punishment for this wanton act had not as yet been meted out, that it remained for him to do so. All other thoughts were quickly displaced.

The ceremonies concluded, Ornon dismissed the gathering and quitted the hall. Dulok hurried through the lengthy corridors to his own quarters, his mentor close at his side. Not a word was shared between them until they were within the confines of the spacious apartment.

"I welcome your return with great joy and great sorrow, Dulok," said Qual affectionately. "It grieves me to have had to relay such news to you."

"If not for your message, old friend, I might have lingered in the City of Gods, such was the headiness of success. But quickly! Tell me all that you know!"

"It is believed that Sallia was taken from the garden," Qual related. "Two guards that might have prevented access were later found dead. But the note on Bori's door leads one to believe that help from the inside would have been necessary, for ingress to the palace is nigh impossible. Bori reported the abduction to Ornon, who was truly concerned, and would have loosed the entire Shadzean army on Blotono. But the note warned against this, threatening any reprisals with Sallia's quick death."

"And you believe that Buz shared in this plot?" Dulok asked.

Qual shook his head. "Of this I have no proof, but he

174

did appear conveniently to offer his services within moments of the discovery of the note."

"How I'd like to put a honed blade to the throat of Lonz and learn what we desire!" Dulok snapped.

"A quick way to forfeit all you have strived for," Qual warned.

"Fear not, mentor," Dulok assured him. "I am no fool. Is it a certainty that Sallia was taken to the City of Rogues?"

"An ambitious fisherman had wandered far south of his appointed grounds, and had made camp on the shore of the Telliun Ocean, near the spot where the Terven Marshes end. He espied a strange vessel, one which he was certain was a privateer. The fisherman concealed himself and his small boat, and for a full day he watched this ship. The privateer anchored close to the shore, and a boatload of sailors was dispatched. These questionable-looking fellows dragged the boat up on the sand and lolled about, obviously waiting for someone. Toward the end of the afternoon a trio of riders arrived, and were greeted by the sailors. Two were men, the other a dark-haired woman of great beauty, according to the fisherman. She was led into the boat, and they rowed toward the larger vessel, all save one of the pair, who returned the way he had come. The woman appeared to be resisting, for she attempted to leap over the side of the skiff; but she was restrained by the boisterous sailors, who treated her roughly. Once all were aboard, the privateer pulled anchor and headed south. The fisherman immediately returned to his home and reported this to the provincial governor, who dispatched a detailed account via messenger hawk."

"Was this known to Ornon before Buz departed?"

Dulok asked.

"No. Buz left the next morning, vowing that he would travel through the Terven Marshes to reach the City of Rogues in all possible haste."

"Then he would surely arrive before the privateer!"

"You know Buz too well by this time, as do I," Qual spat. "He journeyed toward the marshes, but once out of the city's sphere he was met by a well provisioned wagon. He transferred to this wagon, which then set off along a path that would bypass the marshes and lead him to the same spot where the privateer was sighted. He no doubt commissioned another vessel to take him south in comfort."

"The swine!" growled Dulok. "With the jutting out of the coastline, and the purported treacherous currents near the shore, such a journey to the City of Rogues would consume nine or ten days! Doubtless he is still in route! What could he expect to do to succor Sallia? He is a craven!"

"He has promised Ornon the head of Blotono," said Qual. "If he indeed has dealings with these rogues, then I believe that they too are falling prey to his wiles. If not, then I fear the wrong man has been sent to rescue Sallia."

"Whatever it might be, it is unimportant," Dulok stated. "All that matters is the safety of Sallia. I will depart in the dark hours, so that few will see. Advise Ornon that I have journeyed to the hills for rest and meditation prior to the day of the Reckoning, as is my right. For now, see that my stallion is well fed and rested. He has been through much, but I fear I must call upon him again. I will sleep now, and will count on you to awaken me."

"But Dulok, you cannot do this!" Qual protested. "To

176

interfere with the Princes' Trial of another is a grievous offense, and could cost you all that you have worked for."

"You would entrust the life of Sallia to one such as Buz, mentor?" Dulok asked. "No, the throne of Shadzea pales by comparison. I would have it no other way."

"Nor I, my prince," stated Qual humbly. "I apologize for my thoughtlessness. I should not have expected you to act differently. Your orders shall be carried out, and I will awaken you at the appointed time. Sleep well, Dulok."

Qual exited the apartment, leaving the troubled prince to his thoughts. But the fatigued Dulok had little time to think. After bathing himself he succumbed to the comfort of his cot, and within seconds he slumbered deeply.

Lonz had quitted the chamber after admitting the shadowy one, for the actions of one such as he were not for the mentor to observe. The other carried a large canvas sack, the contents of which would have made Lonz shudder. They had decided, due to the absence of the first son, to place matters in their own hands, at least for the time being.

The hour was late, and the corridors were deserted. Lonz found a chamber that he knew to be vacant, and it was there he chose to remain. He knew that it would not take long.

The normally alert Dulok had to be shaken vigorously, so deep was his slumber. He would have leaped up, but Qual gently restrained him. He saw the face of his kindly mentor, and he smiled.

"My own journeys have apparently taken their toll," he admitted.

"You are certain that you are up to this?" asked the concerned Qual.

"Were I not, I would still not linger here," the prince replied.

"I have left this question unspoken until the end, for I fear the answer," offered Qual hesitantly. "You journey through—through the Terven Marshes?"

"Why ask that which you already know the answer to, mentor? You yourself taught me that years ago. If I am to assist Sallia, then I must arrive there in all haste. By following the paths of others I will achieve nothing. Only by crossing the Terven Marshes can I gain any advantage over them."

"But the Terven Marshes—!" began Qual.

"—can offer no worse than the Forest of Sothor," Dulok interrupted, "and I have already survived that accursed place. Fear not, Qual, for I shall return again."

"Often in the past you have said that, and yet this time—" Qual's sentence went unfinished.

"This time, what?"

"This time I fear I—shall never see you again. I don't know why I should feel this way, but I do nonetheless."

Dulok laughed heartily and slapped the mentor on his shoulder. "You are not rid of me yet, Qual. Keep everything in readiness, for we must begin preparations for the day of the Reckoning. Farewell, mentor."

"Farewell, Dulok," replied Qual sadly. "May Doj and Bao keep you safe, and may they return you quickly."

The two clasped hands, and Dulok departed the chamber after scooping up his weapons. Qual slumped to the cot, his head down, and he pondered the hardships of the two young people who meant so much to him. Why had the gods chosen them, above all others, to be put to the test so often? They loved each other, and this should be enough to sustain them throughout their lives. The curse of their birth hung heavy on them, as he well knew.

Qual remained in Dulok's apartment long after the prince had departed, for the thoughts that troubled his mind were unrelenting. He did not know why he felt what he did, but the sensation was strong. He regretted informing Dulok of his fears, for the prince had many other things to trouble himself with.

The first time he noticed the dense, reddish mist that swirled in slowly under the door was when a hidden sense advised him of a nearby presence, a presence unlike anything within his sphere of understanding. He turned his head slowly, and upon seeing the vapor he rose mechanically to his feet. He strode to the door, unafraid, for he knew that the time had come. The mist continued to pour in, until a great mass filled the chamber directly in front of him. Slowly, inexplicably, the cloud altered its form and texture, and where once there was smoke there now stood a creature, a huge, silent beast with taloned paws and rending fangs; a creature summoned from the blackest depths of a crazed soul to perform its brief nocturnal work.

The lone guard heard the piercing scream, and he raced through the corridor to locate its source. Within seconds he had arrived at the door of the prince's apartment. Perhaps it was the lateness of the hour, or the poor lighting in the hall, but the normally sharp-eyed soldier did not notice the last vestiges of red mist disappearing around a nearby corner. His concern was with what had transpired within the confines of the room. He rapped sharply three times, and upon receiving no answer he took it on himself to investigate. The door was jammed, for something heavy lay against it on the other side. He forced an opening wide enough to pass through, and he entered the apartment. When he saw the scene his senses reeled, and he fought to retain consciousness. The bulk of Qual's remains lay by the door, while all across the room were scattered entrails and various organs.

The old mentor had been torn to pieces.

CHAPTER THIRTEEN

THE MARSH HERMIT

Dulok followed the same path as Buz toward the Terven Marshes, but unlike his deceitful half brother there was no rendezvous for him along the way. The perimeter of the marshes, though not a far distance from the City of Kings, could not be reached for a day and a half. There were no roads, the hills were numerous, and the journey across a wide savanna was made difficult by the countless thorny shrubs that covered every square foot of ground. Though overburdened with the knowledge that time was of the essence, Dulok nevertheless took great care in protecting his steed from any risk of serious injury.

By mid-afternoon of the second day, the terrain had begun to alter appreciably. The hard, dusty earth of the plain had softened to a rich loam. Dry shrubs gave way to green and purple ferns, as well as to strange trees with wide, colorful fronds. Dulok knew that he had reached the edge of the Terven Marshes, and for the first time a wave of apprehension swept over him. But just as quickly it passed, for he knew what he must do. With a decisive pressing of his heels he urged his nervous stallion onward.

As he rounded the base of a low hillock, Dulok noticed a small, ramshackle building less than fifty yards away. A slight smile crossed his face as the memory of childhood nightmares was brought to mind. He and the other young princes, as a deterrent to mischievousness, were often told the tale of the Marsh Hermit, a horrid fiend who lurked on the edge of the Terven Marshes. The descriptions given of the Marsh Hermit by the mentors would send their charges into fits of shuddering, at the same time temporarily saving the mentors from any new pranks the princes might concoct to annoy them with. The sight of the broken-down hovel had rekindled that spark of memory in Dulok's brain, and for a moment he paused to reflect on it.

Neither horse nor rider were aware of the intruder, for the rider was lost in thought, while that which approached was downwind from the steed's keen sense of smell. Dulok decided to travel away from the shack, for he had no idea what to expect. He wheeled the stallion about, and there, less than ten feet in front of them, stood the intruder on four paws. It was no bigger than a small dog, and had some canine features, but there was little doubt that it was reptilian. Its greenish, leathery skin was covered with scales, while its tail was pointed and immobile. At the end of each of its four paws were two curved nails, indicating that it might be arboreal. In its mouth, cavernous for its size, were rows of small razorlike teeth. It made no audible noise.

All this had taken the surprised Dulok only seconds to absorb, but it afforded him little time to calm his horse. The fidgety stallion reared high in the air at the sight of this compact monstrosity, and Dulok was hurled to the ground, where his head struck a rock. He was able to see the horse flee before blackness overcame him.

A vague whinnying could be heard, as if a horse were a considerable distance away. There was much throbbing, a dull, heavy thud within the stunned man's head. He opened his eyes, and at first he thought that night had fallen, for he could not see. But light was definitely passing through, and he realized that things were blurred. He rubbed his eyes and shook his head, but when he reopened them he was sorry that he had. The small horror that he had first seen on the ground in front of his horse was only inches from his face, sniffing him curiously. Its seeming placidity did not diminish its grotesque features, and at the thought of it being so near, the dazed fellow leaped to his feet and shouted. The tiny beast, frightened by the man, squealed loudly and ran. It leaped into the arms of another, who cuddled it and spoke soothingly to it.

"You shouldn't go scaring Essa like that, young fellow," a rasping old voice admonished. "She's just a little thing, and quite sensitive."

"Who—who are you?" Dulok dropped to one knee, for his head throbbed mercilessly from the blow he had received. "What is that thing?"

"Essa? Why, she's a marsh feerith. Found her just recently, when she was no bigger than my fist. She'd been orphaned, so I decided to raise her myself. As for me, well, I forgot my name a long time ago, just like I forgot all the people that I came here to get away from. I've been called many names since, and not all complimentary. One I like, though, was the Marsh Hermit. Call me that or

183

call me nothing; it's of no mind to me."

Dulok again rubbed his strained eyes before attempting to further explore his surroundings. He saw that he was within the confines of a hut, probably the small building that he had observed from a distance. It was still daylight, for he could see through a small door to the outside, where his stallion stood quietly awaiting him.

The dazed young prince suddenly leaped to his feet again, much to the surprise of the other. It had taken many moments for the man's words to register in his dulled brain, but it occurred to him that the fellow had called himself the Marsh Hermit. Whether he spoke in jest or not the prince was unable to tell, but the nightmares of his childhood had become quite real to him.

"I have no intention of devouring you, son, if that's what's making you jumpy," the fellow rasped. "I don't even eat the animals around here, just berries, tubers, thing like that. I started that Marsh Hermit talk long ago, before I left the city, to keep people away. Sure has worked through the years."

The man approached Dulok, who remained on the alert. For the first time the prince was able to study his host, and he was amazed by what he saw. The fellow was quite old, but whether he was seventy, or twice that, Dulok could not tell. He was naked, save for a loincloth woven of frond fibers, and his wiry body denoted strength and vitality. When he smiled he showed a mouthful of unbroken white teeth. He had lengthy white hair, but his facial whiskers were short and well trimmed. His eyes were soft and friendly, and Dulok found it impossible to fear this man, nor to bear suspicions of him.

"It was you who brought me here, I presume?" asked the prince.

The old man nodded. "I saw you fall from your horse, but I was too far off to warn you. Essa had run on ahead of me, because she was hungry." He ruffled the leathery head of the beast, who purred ecstatically.

"Allow me to thank you for helping me," Dulok offered. "My name is—"

"Please!" snapped the old man. "I care little for who you are, for you will not pass this way again. Be you prince or beggar, it matters little to me."

"As you wish," Dulok replied. "Now, what are your plans for me?"

"Plans? For you?" the old man exclaimed. "I have no *plans* for you. You are free to leave, if you wish. Your steed is outside. If you desire to stay and rest for the night, you may. I do not care."

"I believe I will remain here, and depart in the morning," said Dulok. He was somewhat annoyed by the old man's attitude, but he knew that the fellow had a right to his privacy. "Is that all right with—?"

But the old man and his feerith slipped silently out the door before the prince could complete his sentence. Dulok staggered to the opening and gazed outside, but the pair was nowhere to be seen. How strange a creature, thought Dulok. And yet, who can fault him for living a life that he chooses, a life that satisfies him? He would leave in the morning, so that the old man might continue his existence without further interference.

The black stallion, none the worse for its experience, was tethered nearby, and it munched happily on some tasty foliage. Dulok spoke a few soothing words to it, and then returned to the hovel. There was a clay receptacle

185

on the floor which was filled with water. Dulok gratefully partook of the liquid, and then slumped to the hard ground. He would have continued his journey, but his head still reeled from the fall. Besides, he reasoned, darkness was falling, and to enter the marshes at night would be folly. He fell asleep that night in the lair of the Marsh Hermit, the horror that mentors would be telling their charges about for centuries to come. But that night there were no nightmares, and he slept undisturbed.

The feerith once again was the first sight witnessed by Dulok upon awakening the next morning. This time he did not alarm the creature, but merely smiled at it. It suddenly entered his fogged brain that where the animal was, so might be the Marsh Hermit. He raised his head and swept the room with his eyes. He was surprised to find the old man seated on the floor only a few feet from him. The normally alert Dulok had not even heard him enter.

"Good morning. I trust you slept well?" Dulok offered.

"I brought you food," said the old man, ignoring the greeting. He pointed to a basket of fruits and nuts, the like of which were unknown to Dulok.

"I am grateful to you," said Dulok, as he took the basket and selected a red-skinned fruit. It was juicy, and quite delicious. "But why did—?"

"Your plans are to travel through the marshes, are they not?" the old man interrupted.

"Yes," answered Dulok. "I journey to—"

"Again I tell you!" the old man snapped. "I care not who you are, nor where you go. I just wish to see you gone. I will tell you things you need to know about the marshes, so that you might survive. Do not take the

186

horse with you, for it will surely die. Leave it with me. I will care for it, and should you live you may come back to claim it. Travel only where the most noise is prevalent. Always be certain to have at least one taok tree within your sight. It is easily distinguishable, for it has a wide trunk and tiny, reddish leaves. And, most important, avoid the red pits! That is all."

The old man rose to his feet and strode to the door, the feerith close at his heels. Dulok looked questioningly at him.

"I find it difficult to understand all that you say," he stated.

"Once within the marshes, you will know," the Marsh Hermit assured him. He stopped near the door and gathered up an object that stood against a wall. "You carry a strong bow?" he asked.

"My bow is among the finest in—!"

"Then you will need this. And this!" The old man tossed the object, which was a quiver of arrows, to Dulok. He then scooped up a coil of heavy cord, which he also threw.

"What will I do with these?" asked the confused prince. But the hermit had already exited, and this time it appeared that he would not be returning.

Dulok turned the quiver around in his hands, discovering that it was not made of leather, but rather from the strands of a very tough, fibrous plant. The arrows presented even more of an engima, for instead of the conventional wooden shafts and steel heads, these darts were manufactured entirely from a singular piece of sturdy black metal, a kind which Dulok had never before seen. The controlling feather near the nock was larger than those of his own arrows. But the most puzzling feature was the eyehole that was welded to the side of the shaft just inches below the nock. What significance could this have? And what use would this cord be against the quantity of thick hemp he had brought? Maybe the Terven Marshes would provide the answer, as the old man had said. But for now, these items only served to further mystify him. He slung the quiver and the cord over his shoulder, and with a shrug he exited the hovel.

The old man was nowhere to be seen, but Dulok was certain that he could not be far off. He strode to the side of the contented stallion and gathered his sturdy bow, as well as his supply of food and water, which he combined with the stores given him by the Marsh Hermit. He crammed his own supply of arrows into the spacious quiver, and after stroking the animal's muzzle he set off on foot into the dreaded Terven Marshes. He loathed leaving the fine beast behind, but he felt certain that the old man was right. He also was confident that the hermit would provide it with good care.

Travel with the noise, the old man had said. But in these marshes, it appeared that to avoid it would be impossible. Insects, birds, and other animals raised their voices in a never-ending cacophony of shrill sounds. When he was fortunate enough to witness some of these birds, Dulok saw rainbows of beautiful plumage that an artist would have been at a loss to duplicate. These marsh denizens scolded the intruder as he passed, and they fled squawking as he laughingly wagged a finger at them.

During the morning hours, Dulok found the passage to be easy. The night's sleep had quelled the throbbing in his head; he had plenty to eat and drink, and the soft, rich soil beneath his sandaled feet had varied little since the outskirts of the marshes. His steed could easily have traversed this ground, and for a moment he felt a pang of regret at leaving the animal. But eventually the earth began to soften more, and the dense foliage converged around him. The footing became treacherous, and his momentum was slowed. The mud would rise to his ankles at times, and there were instances when he thought that he would not be able to free himself. But each time he did, and he continued to plod forward.

Taok trees were numerous in this part of the marsh, as were many fruit-bearing trees. Some bore fruit of a kind given to Dulok by the hermit, and this helped assure the prince that he would not starve here. It was at the foot of a thick taok tree that Dulok spent his first night in the Terven Marshes. He had covered only a few miles that day, and he chafed bitterly at his inability to hasten the journey. He prayed that the going would be better the next day, or at least no worse.

CHAPTER FOURTEEN

THE RED PITS

The second day of the trek through the Terven Marshes offered little relief to the Shadzean prince, whose concern for the safety of Sallia increased with each new obstacle. The mire that slowed him grew deeper, the swamp grasses that emerged from it more dense. Slowly, painstakingly he propelled his tired body through the mud, but by the early part of the afternoon he was exhausted. Still he continued, for to halt in the grasping bog would be to court death. Not until late in the day, when he hauled himself atop a welcome patch of firm ground, did he crumple in a heap and allow himself the luxury of catching his breath.

Dulok was to find his respite short-lived, for the bog that had retarded his progress also produced a new danger, a subtle danger that could not have made itself known until this moment, when he was free of it. He had long since discarded all his garments, save for a thin breechcloth, for the marshes were hot and steamy, even at night. Now he could see that his mud-encrusted body was dotted with large, bloodsucking insects. He leaped to his feet and attempted to brush them off, but they could not be dislodged, for most had attached themselves tightly to this unexpected and welcome source of food. The smaller ones were colorless, while the larger of them, those that had ridden the longest, were bloated and purplish, each thicker than a man's thumb. Although on the verge of panic, Dulok withdrew one of his arrows from the quiver, and with the edge of its razor-sharp head he began to slice each of the parasitical vermin in half, lengthwise. Those that had engorged themselves spurted copious amounts of blood in the air, and Dulok was repulsed, for he knew that it was his own. After long, painstaking minutes the last of them dropped to the ground, and with the toe of his sandal he propelled each squirming half into the mire that had spawned it.

The prince once again dropped to the ground, fatigued by his efforts and weakened by the loss of blood. Though his appetite was nil, he knew that he must eat in order to maintain his strength. He absently gnawed at a quantity of nuts, but when he bit into one of the fruits he discovered that it had rotted. Disgustedly he emptied his pouch of the soft remains and hurled them into the bog. He could easily have plucked fresh fruits from the nearby trees, but he did not wish to expend the effort. He contented himself with the nuts, which he washed down with large swallows of water.

The thin rays of the setting sun filtered down through the overhanging moss and creepers that encompassed the Terven Marshes. Dulok awakened with a start, for in the hour preceding sunset he had fallen into a deep, troubled sleep. In his dreams he had undergone excruciating tortures at the hands of unspeakable swamp denizens, creatures that paled the very demons of Esh. The dreams disturbed him, and despite the warmth of the sultry night, he shivered. He decided that the overhanging boughs of a nearby taok tree would offer him security until morning, and without further thought he plodded to the base of the thick bole to begin his ascent.

Dulok's fevered brain initially prevented him from fully comprehending what occurred next, so quickly did it come to pass. His head had disappeared above the lowest of the leafy branches, when a whirlwind of savage fury lashed out at his unprotected face. In an effort to protect himself he lifted his hands, and his hold on the tree was lost. He plummeted to the ground, and only the soft loam saved him from any serious injury. He quickly felt of his face, and, though his vision was clouded by crimson, he knew that he had somehow been miraculously spared the loss of his eyes. However, he had received more than one painful laceration of the scalp, and a portion of his left ear had been torn away.

His examination took only seconds; but in this time Dulok's unseen attacker descended the bole, and with a vicious scream it leaped at him. Dulok raised his hands instinctively, and he found himself clutching the tough, leathery hide of some marsh denizen. Sharp fangs bit into his left hand, and with a cry of pain the prince hurled the beast from him. He rose quickly to his feet and wiped the accumulated blood from his eyes. Before him, screeching wildly, stood a marsh feerith; but unlike the tiny, gentle one the old man kept as a pet, this creature was fully grown, and it was clearly a formidable force of destruction. It weighed more than fifty pounds, and stood taller than Dulok's knee. Saliva poured from its slavering jaws, and it snarled menacingly at this unwanted intruder.

Dulok had drawn his sword, awaiting another attack by the creature, when a second one fell from above and lit on his back. The prince, reacting quickly, dropped to the ground and pinned the beast beneath him. The feerith, stunned by the blow, relinquished its hold on Dulok, who was able to regain his feet at the moment the first creature hurled itself through the air at his face. Dulok thrust his sword out in front of him and skewered the beast, who screeched violently before expiring. After freeing his blade from the carcass he wheeled to face the other. The injured feerith had limped to where the intruder stood, and before Dulok spotted the thing it had sunk its fangs into his ankle. With a cry of pain he swung his heavy blade and clove the head of the feerith from its glistening torso. The body fell away, but the teeth remained lodged in the prince's flesh, the result of some obscene reflex. Dulok was forced to pull the spurting head from his leg, and this pain was even more grievous.

Darkness now pervaded the marsh as Dulok went about the business of depositing the carcasses into the deep bog. He realized that it was he who had disturbed these arboreal creatures in their nest, that they were merely protecting what was theirs. He dared not climb that tree, nor any other, for no doubt there were many of them.

After ridding his sanctuary of the reptiles, he tried as best he could to care for his wounds. He bathed the lesser

193

cuts with mud after washing them out, and with the more serious gashes on his arms and legs he used the hermit's cord to stanch the flow of blood. He then reclined on the soft earth, far from any trees, and slept. He feared no further attack, or perhaps he did not care; it was difficult to say.

The next day the injured prince re-entered the clutching mire and continued his endless journey, but within hours he had again reached his limits. The mud was softer now, and deeper. His flailing appendages could not advance him forward, nor could they prevent another disaster that he had realized only moments before was transpiring: he was sinking! The mud was already up to his waist, and with each second he was pulled further down.

It is hard to say why one, so near death, suddenly sees things more clearly than those who have fortunately avoided it. The secret that had stymied Dulok suddenly became as evident as the mud that held him. He tied one end of the hermit's cord to his wrist, and he threaded the other through the eyehole of a metal arrow. While tying the cord tightly to the arrow, he looked around him for a taok tree. He saw one at some distance, but even closer was a clump of fruit trees. The arrow was nocked, the bowstring drawn back with as much strength as he could summon. Deep into the bole of the thickest tree flew the dart, the force so great that only inches protruded without. Dulok pulled in the slack from the cord, and slowly, with agonizing effort, he hauled himself from the muddy death that beckoned him.

The immense effort that Dulok was exerting enabled him to gradually raise himself from the mud, but this same force dislodged the metal arrow from the fruit tree, and the prince again began to sink, this time more rapidly. The bark of this tree was too pulpy to sustain any weight, which brought to light the importance of the taok. Dulok twisted his body toward the nearest one. Though at some distance he knew that he could reach it, and there surely was sufficient cord. He hastily reeled in the arrow, and before the mud rose to his chin he again let it fly. This time it lodged halfway into the trunk. He cautiously tested the arrow, finding that it held tightly.

Dulok's chin sat atop the surface of the mire when he began to pull himself out. Hand over hand he struggled, the cord digging into his flesh; but after a few tense, exhausting minutes he had pulled himself free of the quicksand. He collapsed on a rotted log near the base of the taok tree, and for long moments he even ignored the parasites that covered his body.

With the use of his long-bladed knife, Dulok was able to dig the precious metal arrow from the hardwood trunk. He examined it closely, finding that it was not damaged in any way. What a fool he had been for not seeing it sooner than he had. How much precious time would have been saved? How fewer risks to his life? He removed the quiver from his shoulder and counted the strange darts that had been given him by the hermit. There were ten in all, surely too few to be wasted haphazardly. But what of the effort expended in their recovery? He had spent much time retrieving the first one, and time was an even more precious commodity. He decided it best to face these decisions as they arose, and after freeing his body of the parasites he resumed his dangerous trek.

The young prince re-entered the ooze that was the carpet of the Terven Marshes, but after minutes of tedious trudging he again found himself unable to move. The swamp was impassable at this point, and it was evident that the only answer was the continuous use of the cord and the arrows. He drove another missile deep into the next taok tree, and once again pulled himself free. After painstakingly removing the arrow, he repeated the procedure over and over. On three occasions his arrow bit so deeply into the bole that he was forced to abandon it, lest he waste more valuable time and expend precious energy.

So it went, for hour after hour. By mid-afternoon he had covered many miles, and his spirits became up-lifted as he visualized an eventual end to this mad journey. His hands hurt him badly, for the cord continued to dig into his flesh. He fashioned makeshift gloves from nearby fronds, and this helped alleviate some of the pain. Fewer and fewer of the bloodsuckers troubled him, for with renewed zeal he was able to pull himself along rapidly.

Only five arrows were left to him as the afternoon wore on, and now Dulok took the additional effort to dig the most recently used one out of the tree. Past this particular taok he noticed that the floor of the marshes took on a new characteristic. The impassable quicksand was behind him, replaced by a soft, albeit walkable loam. How long it would last he could not tell, but he was determined to cover as much ground as possible. Leaving the sixth arrow where it was, he leaped the short distance over a deep mud pit. His sandals sank into the yielding earth, but no more than an inch, and this from the impact of the jump. He strode forward purposefully, pleased with his good fortune.

Travel with the noise. Once again the words of the Marsh Hermit pounded at his brain, and he knew why. It had happened so slowly, so gradually that there was no way he could have noticed, so intent had he been on his efforts over recent hours. The manifold sounds of the marsh had abated drastically, until now he stood in the midst of absolute silence. He heard no insects, no squawking birds. He cast a small stone upward into the dense foliage of a tree, but no denizen objected to this intrusion. He was alone, more alone than he had ever felt before, and the mere implication caused him to shudder in the heat of the day.

The first of the red pits appeared on Dulok's right. From a distance it looked no different than the numerous mud holes that pocked the marshes. But as he stood over it Dulok saw that, instead of the rich brown mud so common here, the mud in this pit was heavily tinged with red. Perhaps the pits contained clay, thought Dulok. Whatever the case, it did not seem to be anything he should greatly fear, as long as he avoided passing through one. He noticed bubbles rising from below and popping on the surface, and the stench that emanated from each burst overwhelmed him. That alone, he reasoned, was just cause for side-stepping these foul holes.

A second pit appeared, then two others. The ground below his feet soon narrowed as he passed between a maze of them, and at times he feared that he would lose his footing and stumble into one. The stench grew worse, and it brought to mind the memory of his wretched days in the City of Madness. He prayed that he would leave them quickly behind.

Dulok did not see the first of them emerge, for it occurred in a pit to his rear. Numerous bubbles appeared on the surface simultaneously, followed closely by a greenish lump. It rose tall in the center of the pit, as if propelled by unseen hands below. This ovoid mound sat atop what appeared to be a thick human torso, had one wished to stretch his imagination beyond the boundaries of reason. A quartet of appendages, each ending in numerous digits, were in the approximate area of human limbs. But there any similarity ended, for this gelatinous, translucent abomination had no face, at least none where a face should be. The bulbous masses on either side of its pseudohead might have been ears, but the location of its visual organs, if any, was unknown. It stepped clumsily onto the soft loam after surfacing, and with lumbering steps it plodded toward the unsuspecting Dulok.

The prince saw the second and third rise simultaneously, and he gasped in horror. With a swift motion he drew his long, deadly sword from its sheath. They were emerging on either side of him, and he was uncertain of where first to turn, but that decision was quickly made for him. He felt the hairs on the back of his neck prickle, and he whirled around to face the silent horror that stood only a few feet from him. The armlike appendage on its right side, nearly twice as long as the other, reached out to Dulok, the tiny digits undulating obscenely. Dulok swung his sword and easily severed the appendage in the middle. The creature remained silent, but it did stop. No blood spurted forth from cut arteries, for the substance of the thing was the same throughout. It tilted its mockery of a head downward, as if studying its severed

198

member. Dulok gazed down at it also, and he saw that the appendage, whether by reflex or the gods know what, was continuing toward him! The digits still gestured as they propelled the rest of the arm along the humus. Dulok swore in disgust, and with a mighty kick he consigned the putrid thing to a nearby pit.

The second and third travesties had quitted their pits, while other holes spewed forth new ones, all in various stages of emergence. Dulok swung his blade fiercely at the two closest creatures. Bits of slime filled the air as they flew in all directions, some even landing on the sickened prince. But still they poured forth from their pits, these silent green obscenities, and they choked the very air that Dulok breathed with their stench. The overwrought prince slashed and hacked at these unrelenting things, whose silence was almost as terrifying as their appearance.

Slowly, with much deliberation, Dulok fought his way through the crush of these horrors. Bits of living tissue were pulverized beneath his sandals, and he could feel the slime seep between his toes. Once he felt pressure on his ankle, and a hasty glance down revealed a many-digited hand clutching at him. He pulled the thing from his leg, and it became pulp in his strong grasp.

Now he hacked away blindly, and with each mighty stroke his strength ebbed further. He feared that he would be unable to withstand much more, when he suddenly noted that the way before him was clear. No more of the red pits stood in his way. Behind him, the manifold pieces of the gelatinous abominations continued to squirm and wriggle, and he saw them crawl back into the holes that had spawned them, there most likely to rejoin themselves. Dulok shuddered at the thought, and with great haste he quitted the vicinity of the red pits. His strength was all but sapped, and he felt that his overwrought mind could not be far behind.

CHAPTER FIFTEEN

ABOARD THE SEA ROGUE

The night was filled with a thousand horrors for the young prince of Shadzea, dark, abysmal horrors of a tormented mind. Manifold shapes crawled from red and black pits to spread their dripping slime across the land. The foul spawn of Esh passed before him, their leering faces and slavering jaws offering promises of unspeakable atrocities. The vicious whips of the Fashaar overseers lashed against his back and shredded his flesh.

Dulok wrenched his battered body awake, and he found that the warm, quiet night offered no more than the reality of peace. He sank to the ground, much relieved. He had staggered an inestimable distance after quitting the terrible red pits, but not until the reassuring sounds of the marshes were again distinguishable did he stop. Now the noisy insects and the squawking nocturnal birds soothed him, and he lingered in the safety of their proximity. The worst was surely behind him, and the City of Rogues could not be far off. There the only enemy was man, and this foe frightened him the least.

The earliest hints of dawn were already evident, and Dulok was glad, for he knew that any further sleep would be impossible. He looked around him for the presence of fruit trees, but there were none; for that matter there were few taok trees, and the foliage seemed to have thinned appreciably. After sipping a small quantity of his rapidly diminishing water he staggered to his feet and resumed the journey.

Hours later, Dulok stood atop a hill and gazed down into a sparse valley. The hard, dusty ground beneath his feet had long since assured him that the rigors of the Terven Marshes were behind him. These unconquered lands were within the realm of Blotono, and Dulok could well understand why no Shadzean monarch ever felt the need to challenge this claim of the pirate chieftain and his ancestors. Surely an army could easily meet death during the treacherous passage.

A tiny village was visible far in the distance. Dulok traversed the declivity and strode toward it. On the way he thought of all he had ever learned regarding the City of Rogues. Landlocked entirely by swampland and mountains, the only true access was the Telliun Ocean. The Shadzeans were not a maritime people, and had no navy to send against the city. Long ago an attitude of live and let live, regarding the privateers, had been adopted by the Survivors. They reasoned that the pirates offered little danger to Shadzea, since they preyed mostly on the galleys of the far-off seafaring nations. Only occasionally did they loot the coastal City of Fishers, as well as a small village or two, but never did they penetrate inland, where the Shadzean forces would be more than a match for them.

Criminals of every ilk came to the City of Rogues, for such was the nature of the citizenry preferred by Blotono. Murderers, thieves, and the like were employed on the privateering vessels, while petty offenders, cutpurses, debtors and such, were given other assignments. Some became merchants and innkeepers in the city, while others were sent to outlying villages to serve as farmers and sheepherders. It was toward such a farming village that Dulok now headed.

At the outskirts of the village was a well-beaten road, and it was behind a cluster of boulders alongside this path that Dulok concealed himself. He had noted a few horses in the village, and he longed to acquire one. But in this land, a land of criminals, the most trivial theft was punishable by death. Even were he not caught, Blotono would be alerted that an enemy was in his midst, and this might not bode well for Sallia. It was best to remain inconspicuous for as long as possible.

A man driving a well laden wagon of hay departed the village, and he made his way along the road. Another, returning from his labors in the fields, encountered this fellow, and they stopped to chat within earshot of Dulok.

"You journey again to the city, my friend?" asked the man on foot. "But wasn't it just the other day—?"

"Three days ago," the driver interrupted. "I find myself going more and more often. The tolls of Blotono are becoming quite burdensome. The last load merely paid the taxes. Perhaps with this one I will see some profit; that is, if his collectors are not afoot in the market this day."

"I grieve with you," the other replied. "After the midday meal I return to the fields, for what else can one do?"

The conversation went on interminably, the two complaining about everything in general. Dulok chafed at this delay, but he was in no position to object. The two finally parted, the driver trying his best to cajole the tired old horse to greater efforts, but not succeeding. Dulok waited until the farmer on foot had disappeared, and with much stealth he approached the wagon. The driver may have noticed the sudden shift in weight as Dulok slipped under the bales, but he was of no mind to investigate. He attributed it to a bump in the road, and his slow journey went on.

The bumpy road and the uncomfortable wagon did little to soothe Dulok's aching body, but his alternatives were scant. For hours the driver monotonously urged his nag on, and once they stopped for a short time while he partook of some food. But eventually the city was reached. The man was idly challenged at the main gate and then passed through, for the guards had seen him many times. The cobblestoned streets rattled the wagon, and Dulok had to bite his lip to keep from crying out in pain. Finally it stopped, and Dulok heard the man call out:

"Where is the buyer?"

"He is inside," another voice answered.

"Go and fetch him for me."

"Fetch him yourself, farmer!"

The driver grumbled, but with the shift of weight in the wagon Dulok knew that he had climbed down. He peered out through the bales, and he saw that the street was nearly deserted. It was late in the afternoon, and many of the businesses were closed for the day. The man that the driver had spoken to lounged in front of an open stall, nearly asleep. Dulok quitted the hay wagon and strode hastily to a narrow alley, which quickly engulfed him. He knew that his unkempt, haggard appearance, his lack of clothing, and his array of arms would surely single him out, even in a place as unsavory as this one must be.

Dulok haunted the alleys of the City of Rogues until the sun was nearly down, but there were few afoot in this particular district, and he was not seen. In a large barrel, half filled with water from a recent rain, he managed to clean himself as best he could. He discovered clothes hung out to dry in the rear of a questionable hovel, and, despite the laws prohibiting theft, he commandeered those few garments that suited his purpose. The pilfering of a few pieces of shabby clothing was unlikely to raise the eyebrows of Blotono.

Though he loathed doing it, Dulok discarded his sturdy bow and the quiver of arrows, weapons he was certain would be out of place here. His long knife was concealed under the pilfered waistcoat, while his sword hung conspicuously at his side. From concealment he had observed citizens walking the streets, and all appeared to be similarly armed. He knew that his dangling sword would not mark him.

The smell of sea air reached Dulok's nostrils, and he guessed that the harbor must be close by. In the dim twilight he quitted the alleys and strode unconcernedly through the city streets. He knew that there was almost no chance of being recognized, nor little possibility of being challenged by any who might be in charge of policing the city. He made his way to the water, for he felt that this was as good a place to start as any.

It was the dinner hour, and the numerous shabby docks of the city were nearly deserted. Small trading galleys were tied alongside the piers, while larger vessels, most likely privateers, were anchored in the deeper water. It was possible that one of the large vessels was Blotono's favored ship, the *Sea Rogue*, but from his vantage point there was no way for Dulok to tell.

A large party of coarse men suddenly appeared, causing Dulok to scamper behind a rundown shanty to avoid detection. Each man staggered under the burden of a heavy wooden crate, while one, obviously the leader, urged them forward with much shouting and imprecations. The crates were hauled to a particular dock, where the bearers quickly deposited them on creaking wood planks. They then began the tedious process of loading the crates into various small boats that bobbed in the water.

"Who is there?" a voice not far from Dulok shouted, and at first he thought that he had been discovered. But the other had not seen him. Instead, he challenged the group on the pier.

"You'd best not delay us, harbormaster," growled the leader. "We bear stores for the *Sea Rogue*, and are hard pressed to load them, for it sails tonight!"

"My apologies, friend," replied the harbormaster meekly, as he arrived at the dock. "I did not recognize you. But why does Blotono sail at night?"

The burly leader shrugged. "An important rendezvous up the coast is all that I can gather. It is not for the likes of us to know, for we merely follow orders. Now, enough talk! We have much to do!"

The harbormaster departed, while the coarse fellow

continued to berate his charges. The skiffs were eventually loaded, and each was rowed far out into the harbor. They made for the most distant vessel, the largest one anchored there. Night had fallen completely, but Dulok was able to follow the light of their torches and ascertain their destination. He waited patiently for nearly an hour while the stores were reloaded onto the privateer. The bearers returned the small boats to the pier and retied them.

"Our labors are finished none too soon, lads," roared the leader. "See! Blotono comes!"

The rogue chieftain strutted onto the docks, an entourage of more than fifty villains to his rear, and as Dulok gazed upon him he understood the awe in which all held the man. Blotono stood two heads taller than six feet, and his great bulk of more than three hundred pounds exhibited little fat. He had garbed in red and black silken garments, but unlike his many followers he wore nothing atop his head, which was shaven bare. His scarred, not unhandsome face bore a short, poorly trimmed beard. He scowled venomously, most surely an ill-tempered fellow.

"Dog! Have you not yet finished with the provisions?" he shouted at his lieutenant, who now cowered before him.

"All—all is in readiness, Captain," the man stammered. "Already we—"

"Silence!" Blotono roared. "We have no time for prattle. Let us make for the vessel. Bring the final piece of cargo forward. It will go with me!"

A strong fellow pushed his way through the assemblage, a canvas sack slung over one shoulder. Though the contents appeared heavy, the villain handled it as if it were a trifle. Dulok gazed at the bag, and he saw that something within moved. Sallia! Surely his beloved was the unfortunate occupant of that sack! He thanked the gods that she still lived, and he would have leaped forth to succor her, but he knew that numerous swords would cut him down.

While the pirates boarded the shaky skiffs, Dulok quitted the docks stealthily. He made sure at all times that the shanty stood between himself and the others. Once away, he traveled in a wide arc past numerous other hovels, until he once again came to the water's edge, some distance from the docks. He dove silently into the chilled water and struck out toward the *Sea Rogue*, nearly half a mile away. The huge privateer teemed with bustling sailors, all making ready for the voyage. Dulok swam most of the final fifty yards below the surface, for he feared discovery. He reached the vessel just as the final boatload of sailors was clambering aboard. No sooner did the last one set foot on the deck than the ship was under way. Dulok managed to find a fortunate handhold on the starboard side, to which he clung tightly. He did not have enough time to scramble over the railing, though even if he had he would surely have been seen, for there were many on deck.

The *Sea Rogue* sailed northwest along the coast for hours. Dulok maintained his hold as best he could, but eventually he found himself tiring. He knew that he would have to do something soon, for his arms were growing numb from the chilling water, and were he to lose his hold he would doubtless be unable to make it to shore. Slowly, cautiously he pulled himself up the side of the vessel. He exercised great care in making as little noise as possible. The hour was late, and as such he prayed that most of the crew had retired. To his relief, he found this to be the case. The deck was nearly deserted, with only essential personnel afoot, each concerned with his own particular task. Dulok topped the railing and fell silently to the deck. He found his way to the hatch of the cargo hold, which was partially open. A hasty glance around assured him that he had not been seen. He lowered himself into the hold, and with a sigh of relief he reclined amongst the stores and caught a momentary breath.

At the far end of the cargo hold was a small door, this leading into a passageway that contained the tiny cubicles used as quarters by Blotono and his chief officers. At the end of the passageway was a worn wooden stairway that led to another part of the deck. Dulok strode the length of the corridor carefully, lest he be discovered; but the blustering and snoring that emanated from behind the door of each small apartment assured him that the occupants slept.

He stopped suddenly at the door of one cubicle, that nearest the stairs, for a faint sound had been detected by his sensitive hearing. It sounded much like—like a woman sobbing! He undid the latch carefully, and the door swung open with ease. There in the corner, her hands and feet bound, was Sallia, his beloved Sallia! In spite of her ordeal she appeared to him more beautiful than ever. She gazed hopelessly at a wall, and she did not hear him enter. He closed the door behind him and knelt at her side.

"Your suffering is nearly at an end, my flower," he

whispered softly.

Sallia turned her reddened eyes quickly, for she had been startled by this unexpected presence. She immediately recognized the battered face of her lover, and she would have screamed for joy had not Dulok clamped his hand over her mouth. He deftly cut the bonds that held her. She fell into his arms and covered his face with kisses, which he gladly returned. With her head buried in his chest she began to sob once more, but this time her tears were not those of despair.

"Often I feared I would never see you again, my prince," Sallia managed to gasp between sobs. "May the gods curse me for ever doubting you!"

"Nothing would have kept you from me, Sallia. I departed the City of Kings shortly after Buz, and—"

"The accursed Buz!" Sallia spat. "Then he too came after me?"

"He chose this as his Trial of Death, along with the return of Blotono's head. But Qual feared duplicity. Besides, I would not have entrusted your life to that dog!"

"But Dulok, you have interfered with his trial!" Sallia protested. "He could have you destroyed for such an act!"

"It doesn't matter, now that you are safe. He has had ample time to succor you, and as yet has not appeared. I will see you safely to your beloved garden."

Dulok peered out cautiously into the narrow corridor, but still found it to be deserted. He took Sallia by the hand and led her to the cargo hold. Once inside Dulok quietly closed the door, and the relieved pair sank to the floor. Sallia smiled at her rugged warrior, and she held him tightly. No further words were necessary, for he had proven to her that nothing, not even the throne of Shadzea, was as important to him as their love. Perhaps one day she would dare broach the subject of leaving the City of Kings for a more simple life in some distant province. Whatever obsession had forced him to strive for his goals could surely not possess him as it had before. Yes, she would wait until their return, and . . .

A gentle collision brought them instantly alert. The vessel had run into something, and even now the creaking of wood indicated that it was rubbing up against the obstacle. Footfalls were heard in the corridor, and a loud knock sounded on the door of the cubicle nearest the cargo hold.

"Who dares disturb my slumber?" roared the angered voice of Blotono.

"Captain," answered another, "the rendezvous has been made. Even now he waits above to speak with you."

"Oh he does, does he?" replied the venomous voice. "Bring the dog here, and I will deal with him! See that his vessel and its crew are closely watched. Go now, all of you!"

One by one the cubicles emptied as the harried officers scurried up the stairs to carry out the will of their leader. Dulok and Sallia sat breathlessly and awaited developments, praying that they would not be discovered. The creaking continued, and Dulok realized that another vessel had pulled up alongside. Footsteps sounded once again, and two men descended the stairs, stopping as they reached the chieftain's cabin.

"He is here, Captain," the underling said.

"Send him in, fool!" Blotono roared. The unknown

211

guest entered the cubicle, closing the door behind him. Their proximity to the cabin allowed Dulok and Sallia to hear their words.

"Ah, welcome, my *friend,*" said Blotono caustically. "It has been a long time since last our paths crossed."

"Your hospitality is most agreeable, Blotono. I too share your joy in our meeting." The tone was oily, and fawning. Dulok and Sallia looked at each other disgustedly. There could be no doubt about it: the voice belonged to Buz!

The greetings of the first son were immediately followed by a crashing noise, as if a struggle was taking place. Dulok listened carefully, for he knew now that Qual had been right, and he wished to learn as much as possible.

"Enough of this false prattle, you dog!" Blotono bellowed. "Your idle boasts far precede you. So you would return with the head of Blotono, would you? It is not enough that I stole the woman for you, and would have allowed you to *bravely rescue* her from under our noses? What were your plans, cur? Would you have knifed Blotono in the back, or perhaps poisoned his wine? In no other way could you have carried it out!"

"P-please, my friend, you are choking me!" Buz gasped. "Ah, that is better. Surely you wrong me, Blotono. Me kill my friend and ally? Certainly not! But Ornon would wish more than merely the rescue of the woman, so I promised your head to satisfy him. I would ask another favor of you, for which you will be paid well. There must be those among your people who you are displeased with. Provide me with the head of one such dog. Those of Shadzea have never seen Blotono, and

212

would not know the difference. They have only the word of the king's son, which is unquestioned in Shadzea."

Dulok and Sallia were appalled by the words being spoken, though to the young prince it was not much of a surprise, for he would have expected no less of his vile half brother. The conversation continued:

"I am no fool, Shadzean pig!" Blotono roared. "But I will let it pass this time, for I approve of your idea. There is one of my crew who deserves nothing less than such a fate. I will have him drugged, so little resistance might be offered you, and you can easily dispatch him. The girl has never set eyes upon me, and will not know the difference. She will verify your story to Ornon, and your future will be assured."

Dulok realized that now would be the time to make his move, for they would soon come for Sallia, and an alarm would be sounded when they discovered the cubicle empty. With Sallia close behind he strode boldly into the corridor. The lone underling remained on watch outside Blotono's door. He saw Dulok approaching, and he went for his weapon.

"What the—!" he started, but a blade through the heart quickly silenced him. Blotono, overhearing the uproar, thrust his head into the hallway, and for his trouble he nearly lost it. Only his reflexes and great agility prevented the blade from severing his glistening skull, but a large chunk of scalp did fly to the planks. With a lightning move he drew his own blade, a weapon on which legends were based, a sword so heavy that an average man was sorely pressed to even lift it. But in the hands of this giant it was naught but a thin rapier.

"I know not who you are, dog," roared the pirate, "but

213

surely you shall pay for this!"

His huge bulk filled the corridor, and with mighty strokes he forced Dulok back. Only the narrowness of the passageway prevented him from landing the kind of blow that he was more than capable of. Dulok desperately parried each stroke, but the strength of the man was forcing him downward. It was only a matter of time before the intimidating weapon would pierce his defenses.

Blotono suddenly froze in his tracks, and his eyes became glazed. He wheeled about, and the prince could see the long dagger protruding from his back, the dagger that Buz had cowardly placed there. Dulok leaped to his feet as Blotono crumpled to the floor, and he would have run his treacherous kin through, for the thought of Buz's deceit had momentarily blinded him from his long-made vows.

Buz shuffled backward and held his palms toward Dulok. "I know these swine better than you, brother," he advised. "Best we forget our differences for the moment and assist each other in fighting our way out, or we shall pay dearly for the death of Blotono."

The fire left Dulok's eyes as he saw the logic of the situation. With a shrug he indicated the door leading to the storage hold.

"Quickly, barricade that door!" he shouted at Buz. "This will disallow them one further means of ingress."

Buz re-entered Blotono's cabin and dragged out a small wooden table, which he propped against the door. His action came none too soon, for the crew, now aware of the situation below, had poured into the hold in an attempt to trap the enemies between them. While they rattled the door futilely, Buz rejoined Dulok at the foot of the small stairway. More of the pirates poured down the steps, but the narrowness allowed only two at a time to descend, and the princes were able to dispatch their foes in individual combat.

Dulok suddenly found himself doing battle alone, but with renewed zeal he was able to ward off the thrusts of the nearest attackers. Behind him he heard Sallia scream, and against his judgement he chanced a quick glance. Buz had returned to the body of Blotono, and with one stroke of the pirate chieftain's terrible sword he had severed his head. He wrapped the dripping thing in the pirate's waistcoat, and after stuffing it into his own garment he rejoined Dulok. Shoulder to shoulder they fought their way up to the deck of the *Sea Rogue*, with Sallia close behind them.

"Little good that head will do you now, *brother*," hissed Dulok as he skewered another of the pirates.

Buz, his hands full with a skillful swordsman, did not reply, but a quick glance sideways told of further deceit being nurtured in his malignant brain. The proximity of Dulok would make it a simple matter to eliminate him. Yes, as soon as the number of their foes had lessened . . .

"I bear the dagger you used on Blotono, and would gladly thrust it into your foul back lest you even look askance of Dulok!" The voice came from the rear, and belonged to Sallia.

The first son rechanneled his efforts, and amidst much spattering of blood the two princes reached the deck of the privateer. The crew of the galley that had borne the treacherous Buz down the coast was likewise engaged with the pirates, and the sheer numbers of Blotono's men

215

was pressing them down. But now, with these two Shadzean fighting machines on deck, the odds turned. The pirates were no match for these expert swordsmen. Fearing for their lives, lacking leadership, they poured over the side of the *Sea Rogue* like frightened rats. A few of the braver ones remained behind, but they were quickly disposed of.

Dulok and Buz stood on deck, panting heavily, their well used blades dripping. Each had suffered many superficial wounds, but neither was hurt seriously. Dulok turned to Buz, and a grim smile creased his face.

"Submit yourself to my custody, treacherous dog, or die here and now!" Dulok ordered.

Buz looked at his hated kin, and he considered a desperate attempt to run him through, but after thinking better of it he dropped his sword to the planks. Sallia scooped it up and joined Dulok at his side. Dulok then looked at the crew of the small galley that bobbed alongside the privateer. The vessel belonged to the people of a small Shadzean fishing village. They did not know the nature of the task for which they had been commissioned by Buz, nor did they know his identity.

"Hear me! No longer will you take orders from this man," Dulok instructed them. "You will return up the coast from where you came, and in the future you will speak to no one of this!"

The crew was all too happy to comply, for to be this far in pirate waters was not to their liking. All returned to the galley, and they pushed away from the privateer. When far enough away they heaved oil lanterns onto the vessel's deck. In minutes the *Sea Rogue*, Blotono's coffin, was engulfed in flames. Dulok and the others watched, until the last vestiges of the once feared ship disappeared below the surface. The crew then positioned themselves at the oars, and the vessel struck out for Shadzean waters.

CHAPTER SIXTEEN

DESPAIR AND LOATHING

The lengthy voyage back to Shadzea would have been interminable for Dulok, had it not been for the presence of Sallia. Buz was confined below, with only the grisly head of Blotono for company, and they were glad to have him out of their sight. For the first time in their lives they were free of the restraints that limited their relationship, and they shared nearly every moment together. They reveled in the smell of the sea air, the gentle rolling of the ship upon the waves; but mostly their joy was in the proximity of one another, and they consummated their love again and again during the ecstatic nights in their utilitarian cabin.

Sallia still could not summon the courage to discuss future plans with her champion, nor did Dulok broach the subject at all. With Buz now out of the way, it would be left for Dulok to do battle with Korb on the day of the Reckoning. Korb, Sallia knew, was a formidable opponent, and Dulok's prevalence was by no means a certainty. If only Dulok would bring it up, she mused, I would be able to further press the issue. But the prince chose to remain silent throughout, and Sallia's thoughts remained in a turmoil. Still, the unrestrained love they shared served to alleviate much of her pensiveness.

The voyage finally ended less than fifty yards off a small village on the Shadzean coast. Dulok, Sallia, and Buz were taken ashore in a small boat, where, after avoiding the curious stares of a few villagers, they remained overnight. The next morning they purchased horses for their journey to the City of Kings. They departed with but a few words to their hosts, and the final part of their long trek was under way.

The journey across the barren Shadzean plains was uneventful, with not even a brigand to disturb the solitude. For most of the way Dulok kept Buz's hands tied behind him, nor did he relieve him of the mouldering, putrid head, despite the pleading of the first son to do so. Sallia could not understand this, for it was unlike Dulok to purposely inflict petty torture, even to one such as Buz. She never questioned him, for she felt certain that he knew what he was doing.

Many days after departing the coast they neared to within ten leagues of the city, and Dulok knew that they would soon encounter the first of the outlying patrols. It was early in the afternoon when he brought the party to a halt. Sallia could not understand the reason for the pause, for they had not overtaxed the mounts that morning, and with few delays they might reach the gates before dark. But she read something in Dulok's demeanor that disturbed her, something that she had noticed there for the past three days. He had spoken less and less to her, and he appeared to be enmeshed in some great and terrible battle raging within him. She feared the worst, and her trepidation was not unwarranted.

Dulok dismounted and drew a knife from his belt. He strode purposefully toward Buz, and the first son's eyes widened, for he felt certain that he was near death. He cried pitifully for Dulok to spare him, but Dulok ignored his mewling and cut the ropes from his wrists. He then returned Buz's sword to him hilt first, and while the astonished first son rubbed the soreness from his wrists, he addressed him:

"You have the head of Blotono, and you have Sallia. Return with them to Ornon, and do as you will!"

He then turned his attention toward the young beauty, whose face had turned a ghastly pale white as she absorbed Dulok's words. Shocked and appalled by this act of her lover, she chose not to allow him the first words.

"Dulok! By the gods, *are you insane?* You would see this swine a hero? Do you think that I would subject myself to such disgrace? Never! I would first descend into the slime of Esh!"

Dulok led Sallia's mount out of earshot of Buz, who could scarce comprehend what was happening; but he chose not to question his good fortune, for gratitude was an attribute unknown to him, and in his malignant brain he was already formulating new misdeeds to assure ascension to the Shadzean throne. Dulok, once assured of their privacy, looked deeply into Sallia's horrified eyes. The hard appearance of his own orbs frightened her, and for the first time she felt as if she did not know him.

"Hear me, Sallia, and do as I say!" His tone was insistent, yet in it she denoted intense beseechment. "You have given me the greatest gift that one could ask for, your love. Know that it is returned in kind. Go with

Buz to Ornon, and allow him to accept the plaudits of the people with your silence. I will leave you now, and not return to the city for awhile. Some day you will understand, this I swear!"

"But Dulok!" she cried. "Think of what he did to me, and to you! What of my shame, of—!"

"Sallia, please, say no more!" he begged, averting his eyes. "What I ask of you is—*so difficult!*" She thought that she detected a sob. "You must do this for me— *please!*"

Before she could speak again, Dulok mounted his steed and sped away, leaving the bewildered girl to gape after him in disbelief. Buz trotted slowly to her side, a mocking smile creasing his vulgar countenance. He gathered up her reins, and in silence they continued on toward the City of Kings.

Dulok wandered across the plains for days; his meanderings appeared to have no purpose, but he eventually found his way to the edge of the Terven Marshes, which he skirted for an entire morning before coming to the hovel of the Marsh Hermit. He could not find his former host, though he called often to him. But the hermit had long since known of his coming, for he found his favored stallion awaiting him, well fed and prepared for the ride home. Dulok left the other steed as a gift for the elder, and astride his fine animal he made his return.

The city was just recovering from the numerous days they had spent feting Buz, who had returned a great hero from his Trial of Death. Inwardly the idea sickened Dulok, but he was glad that Sallia had kept her silence. The head of Blotono had been preserved and hung in the plaza for all to see. Buz's exploits spread through the city like sagefire, and all were fascinated by the horrors that he encountered in the Terven Marshes, not to mention his harrowing brush with death during his combat with the pirate. The feat of Korb was forgotten in light of this new hero, while the deeds of Dulok had far been overshadowed by a tragic, most shocking development.

Not until he reached the city did Dulok learn of the death of Qual, his mentor and friend. Though stunned and saddened, he was more surprised to find that most believed him to be the perpetrator. All evidence was against him. Qual had been found in Dulok's own apartment; only one of unbounded strength could have destroyed the body in the manner it had been found; and what of his disappearance shortly after? It was his right as a prince of Shadzea to sequester himself after his Trial of Death; but still, it was most convenient. True, all this evidence was circumstantial, and as such his right to continue his quest for the throne of Shadzea could not be taken from him. But all had accused him in their minds, and he fell low in their esteem. Buz had become the champion, and all would laud his success.

Eight months would pass before the day of the Reckoning, and for Dulok they would be the most difficult days of his life, more torturous than any of the previous Princes' Trials he had endured. Sallia refused to see him, and though he would wait in the garden for hours, she would not appear. He would pound on the door of her apartment, but no answer would come from within. He would try and talk to Bori, her father; but the counselor mourned the death of his friend Qual, and he loathed Dulok, for he too believed all that had been said. Friendless, hopeless, the saddened prince would sit alone in his room for hours, and he would pray for it all to end.

Sallia was aware of Dulok's desire to see her, but she could not face him. True, she had kept her silence regarding Buz's treachery, but whether she did it initially for the love of Dulok she could not tell. Now, after time had passed and she had witnessed the adulation of the cowardly Buz, she knew that such was not the case. The shame that she felt was immense, and she loathed Dulok for subjecting her to it. She prayed that Korb would destroy them both, and that she would not be forced to become the queen of either.

But such was not to be, for two months before the day of the Reckoning, the eighth son received a visitation in the night. This time there were many who heard the screams, and when they arrived at his chamber they found Korb in a state similar to that of Qual. Ornon was summoned, and he instantly led the guards to the apartment of Dulok. They threw open the door and poured into the room, only to find the prince asleep on his cot. Dulok went to draw his sword, for at first he did not recognize his assailants, but his arms were pinioned tightly by the overwhelming numbers.

"Sire, what is the meaning of this?" he demanded, as the guards examined his body.

"You just returned to this room?" Ornon insisted.

"I have been asleep here for hours. Why do you trouble me?"

The captain of the guard shook his head, indicating there to be no evidence that Dulok had recently been engaged in a bloody scuffle. He was released, but the soldiers still gazed suspiciously at him.

"Korb is dead," announced the captain, "as if *you* did not know."

Dulok said nothing, but instead gazed into his father's eyes. Ornon had expected to see the fearful look of the accused, but instead he read the knowing eyes of the incriminator. He quickly turned away, and with a sharp command he ordered his men from the room. Dulok returned to his cot, and despite the agonies of his tortured mind he forced a grim smile, for the end of the lifelong charade was drawing nearer.

Fifteen days before the day of the Reckoning, the dignitaries began to arrive. Provincial governors, village elders, and red priests streamed into the city for this infrequent, most historical event. The tide brought Ayo and Turnivo to the palace, and Dulok was thankful for their company, for they were the only ones who knew, the only ones who understood. They spent hours discussing future plans, if indeed there was to be a future, and Dulok's spirits were again uplifted. His confidence, despite the feelings of the populace, was slowly being restored.

The young prince slept soundly on the first night following the arrival of his friends. His dreams were not as troubled as they had been; or so he thought, until he saw the red mist that poured slowly under his door. He rose mechanically from the cot, and without fear he approached the visitor, which was taking shape before him. But before the talons could rake his flesh, before the fangs could rend, the door burst open. There, like a terrible arm of vengeance, stood Turnivo, the priest's son, and high above his head he held the Stone of Bao! The jewel gleamed in the flickering torchlight, and it sent forth its stream of death into the hulk that was the night demon. Where once stood an engine of death, only a small, charred spot remained on the wooden floor.

"Turnivo!" cried Dulok, as his senses returned. "By Doj, what has happened?"

"Though Sothor be destroyed, his acolytes still infest the land," Turnivo replied. "When I learned of Qual and Korb I feared that such was the case, and I knew that you would need further protection. But not until the other day could Ayo remove the stone from its place of rest, for it took time to produce a duplicate. Even so, I found myself asleep only moments ago in my quarters. A stranger rapped on my door and awakened me, or you would surely have died. I have no idea who it might have been."

"You brought the Stone of Bao?" Dulok gasped. "You know what you risk?"

"No more than you have risked in the past, my friend. Now come, for the work of the stone shall be completed this night!"

Turnivo concealed the amulet in his robes, and together the two strode the silent corridors of the palace. As they neared the apartment of Buz each experienced a similar feeling of aversion, as of something evil permeating the air. They quickly shook off the spell, for there was work to be done. Dulok had confidence in his companion, and while he did not know what awaited them, he felt a sense of security.

Dulok slowly opened the door to Buz's chamber, as Turnivo had instructed him to. Instantly he saw what was occuring in the center of the room, and he was repulsed by the sight. Buz sat on the floor, as did another, a cowled figure. Between them was a small globe, which radiated a crimson glow. Both men undulated idyllically, as if they were experiencing ecstasy from the evil power that their minds were generating. Neither heard the prince and his friend enter.

"Bao, I send you one more, for what I pray is the last time!" Turnivo intoned, as he again raised the stone above him. The glow from the ball died, and Buz became aware of others in the room. He opened his eyes, and he immediately espied the charred, smoking spot on the floor across from him. His eyes widened in terror, and he cringed as he stared at the two vengeful occupants of his chamber.

Dulok drew his sword and slowly approached the quaking Buz. He lifted the blade high above his head, but before assigning it downward he turned slightly, and the metal shattered the globe into thousands of shards. He then sheathed the sword and turned to leave. Turnivo followed him out. But the prince's business was not finished, and for the last time he turned to face Buz.

"Your final option has been exhausted, *brother!*" His tone was caustic. "It will now be decided in the courtyard. Enjoy what time is left to you."

The door closed behind the two as they departed, and the terrible night was over.

CHAPTER SEVENTEEN

THE DAY OF THE RECKONING

The few remaining days preceding the final conflict passed quickly. Dulok did not for a moment underestimate the treachery of Buz, nor was his caution in vain. Lonz employed various mercenary assassins in a last desperate attempt to see the sole obstacle to his charge's ambitions eliminated. With the mentor's help these villains were assisted into the palace, and not a night passed without at least one attempt made on Dulok's life. But Turnivo and Ayo, who now shared Dulok's spacious quarters by his own invitation, kept a constant vigil over their friend, and one by one the attempts were thwarted. The bodies of the would-be murderers were disposed of secretly, as per Dulok's request, lest anyone learn of the deceit of the first son.

On the third day before the ultimate confrontation, Buz and Lonz paced the prince's chamber worriedly. It was past midnight, and the time that the latest assassin was to return to collect his well-earned fee had come and gone. Neither uttered the words, but both were certain of another failure.

"You are the eternal wise one, *mentor*," Buz growled. "What are we to do now? The time grows short!"

"Could I have foreseen the trouble he would cause, I would have destroyed him in his youth!" the mentor snapped. "May the gods—"

"May the gods silence your tongue, old fool!" Buz spat. "Your prattle will not help us now. I must face him in the courtyard, and no trickery will be possible before the assembled eyes of Shadzea!"

The two continued to argue ceaselessly, but the futile words they spoke did not fall on their ears alone. A small, robed figure stood just outside the door in the silent corridor, and with a grim smile this person absorbed all that was said. A hand emerged from the folds of the robe, and three sharp raps were sounded on Buz's door. Who would come at this hour, each thought, save the hired assassin? Then perhaps his mission was a success after all! Buz strode happily to the door and admitted the night caller. The figure glided in hastily, and when the door had been closed, the hood was removed.

"Dhela!" Buz gasped, as he recognized the stunning, long-haired young woman. "Why are you here at such an hour?"

"I have been at your door for many minutes," she replied huskily, "and I know what transpires in your mind. Fear not, for I have no intention of revealing your thoughts or actions. I have come to assist you."

"But why would *you* wish to help me?" asked Buz suspiciously. "You fumed when I did not select you."

"It was because I did not understand why you would have chosen the other. Eventually I came to understand that your loathing for Dulok far exceeded all else, and that your choice was made to spite him. Now, with Korb dead, my sole chance to share the throne is gone, and for this I too despise Dulok, for I am certain that it was he who destroyed Korb. I would see him dead before he attains Survivor! You are committed to your choice; but who knows? Perhaps some day you will remember the kindness of Dhela."

She had slowly removed the bulky robe as she spoke, and Buz gazed hungrily upon her shapely form, accented as it was by the tight-fitting scanty garments she wore.

"Your interest is noteworthy," Buz drooled, "but what could *you* do to help assure me the throne?"

"See!" answered Dhela, holding up a tiny phial of greenish fluid that had been clutched tightly in the palm of her hand. "I have gone to great lengths to acquire this deadly poison. A mere touch upon one's skin and death is almost instantaneous. You wonder how you might deceive the eyes of Shadzea in the courtyard three days hence? A few drops on the tip of your sword will be all that you require!"

His hand shaking slightly, Buz accepted the phial from the treacherous beauty. He smiled wickedly at Lonz, and the ecstatic mentor returned the joy in kind. In the midst of their elation they did not see Dhela glide to the door, her robe again donned. But before she could exit Buz noticed her, and he called after her:

"Woman! Be it known that my gratitude is unbounded. The fifteenth Survivor shall not forget what you have done for him."

Dhela nodded silently to the prince, and in an instant she had exited. But before departing she again stood at Buz's door and listened to the voices within as they laughed heartily. She too smiled broadly, for she was well pleased with her night's work.

*　　*　　*

On the final nights preceding the day of the Reckoning Dulok and his friends expected the worst, but to their surprise the time passed uneventfully. Ayo had even reported that he had come across Buz in the courtyard one afternoon, practicing his swordsmanship in earnest. The actions of Buz and his mentor were evident to all, and it appeared that no further deceit was in the offing.

"Perhaps he has exhausted his options after all, as you said," Turnivo stated to Dulok on the morning preceding the final day. "He appears resolved to settle this in the courtyard, in the proper manner. You told me that he has always been a fine swordsman. You are positive that you can best him?"

"It is the least of my concerns," replied the confident Dulok. "But as I've said before, do not underestimate him. He is black-hearted, and I doubt that his bag of tricks has run dry. He would not accept his fate with such resignation."

But the day passed, and darkness fell over the City of Kings as it prepared nervously for the following morning, when the event that occurred so infrequently would come to pass. Dulok lay idly on his cot and stared at the beams that crisscrossed the ceiling above him. Ayo and Turnivo lounged near the door, and both felt concern for Dulok as they gazed at him. They knew that he was well prepared physically, for Turnivo, quite skilled with the sword for the son of a priest, had worked with him. But there was much that disturbed his mind, and the two did not know how greatly this could affect the outcome.

The wise Ayo had been able to glean much during his short tenure in the City of Kings. That evening he

230

excused himself, claiming a desire for a stroll and a breath of air. He found his way to the palace garden, where he seated himself upon a marble bench and waited patiently.

Sallia could not understand why a red priest would desire an audience with her, but out of respect she dared not refuse a holy man of Shadzea. She wrapped a shawl around her shoulders, for the night was chilled, and the priest had chosen the garden, of all places, for their rendezvous. She opened the door slowly, and for the first time in many months she entered the beautiful garden that she had once loved. The priest rose formally and greeted her. He then beckoned her to sit next to him, and in a hushed whisper he spoke for more than an hour.

The sharp knocking on the door pierced the deathly stillness of the chamber. Turnivo leaped to his feet, but he did not draw his blade, for the three short and two long raps was the prearranged signal of Ayo. Turnivo cast open the door, and there stood a beautiful, tearful young woman. Behind her, in the corridor, was his father. The woman nodded at Turnivo as she entered the chamber, and Dulok rose from his cot as his eyes fell upon her. The bewildered Turnivo gazed at Ayo, who motioned him from the apartment with a curt gesture of the head. Sallia, the tears streaming down her cheeks, raced toward Dulok and flung herself into his arms. The uncomprehending prince held her tightly, but said nothing.

Ayo and his son patrolled the corridor for nearly two hours, before the door to Dulok's chamber once again opened. The elderly priest proffered his arm to the radiant young woman who emerged, and with a broad smile he escorted her back to her own quarters. The confused Turnivo re-entered the chamber and gazed upon the prince, but the doleful Dulok that he had left some hours past was no longer there. In his place stood a smiling, confident young man, one who appeared quite ready to face the challenges that the next day would bring. Turnivo smiled inwardly at the wisdom of his father, for he too now understood.

The morning was dark and overcast, but the fiery orb that brought the day offered frequent hints that its presence would be noted before the afternoon arrived. All was in readiness in the courtyard, as it had been for days. Semicircular bleachers had been constructed to accommodate the numerous witnesses, and their positioning about the yard gave the effect of an amphitheater. A special box, reserved for Ornon and other dignitaries, was made more prominent by its plush chairs, a contrast to the hard wooden benches that the others would share. But none would complain, for this was the day of the Reckoning, an historical day for the kingdom, and those in attendance felt themselves fortunate.

The bleachers had been filled for hours prior to Ornon's arrival about mid-morning, all wishing to select the best possible vantage point. Sharing the box with Ornon were Otessea, the queen, the members of the council, and Sallia, she who would be the future queen regardless of the day's outcome. The sly Dhela, though no longer in consideration, also occupied the box, this by request of Otessea. Ayo and Turnivo shared a section of benches with a contingent of red priests from the City of Gods.

Dulok entered the courtyard first, accompanied only by Tirri, who bore his sword. It was the right of the

232

mentor to second his charge, but the unfortunate Qual could only share the courtyard in Dulok's heart that day, one more tally on the score that was to be settled. A low murmur arose at the appearance of the twentieth son, and despite the presence of the king, a few tentative jeers could be heard. But the memory of the cruel deaths of Qual and Korb were too much to bear, and soon nearly all were voicing their disapproval of this would-be Survivor. Sallia shuddered as the venomous taunts were hurled from around her, but a look at her staid warrior gave her renewed confidence.

The first son strutted boldly into the courtyard, with Lonz close behind. The crowd roared their approval at his appearance, and Buz reveled in the joyous reception. He pranced about the courtyard and waved to the gathering, and when he espied Dhela in the king's box he smiled broadly at her. She acknowledged the smile in a like manner. He then returned to the side of the courtyard where Lonz awaited him, and together they stood by for the initiation of the proceedings.

Ornon rose to his feet and held his hands up. The crowd silenced instantly. He gazed intently at all the gathered witnesses, and then he spoke:

"Observed by Boga, the first Survivor, and Dain, the second Survivor . . ." and so forth, through his own father, Nhob, whom he purposely included, though this Survivor never saw the day of the Reckoning in his rule. None chose to correct him. He continued: "Now observed by myself, Ornon, the fourteenth Survivor and king of Shadzea! We have come to this day of the Reckoning with only two princes, one of whom will become the fifteenth Survivor, later to rule all of Shadzea. They are Dulok my twentieth son—" Jeers and catcalls. "—and Buz, my first son!" The crowd broke into ecstatic shouting, and Ornon was again forced to silence them. "Will the princes approach the box?"

Dulok and Buz strode purposefully toward their father. Each wore no clothing save for a thin breech-cloth, this to prevent the concealment of any additional weapons. Only one sword would be allowed each participant. Buz grinned wickedly at his half brother, but Dulok chose to ignore him, and this infuriated Buz. He would take even greater pleasure in disposing of his hated foe. The two reached the box, and they bowed their heads in the presence of the king.

"In a matter of minutes, or perhaps hours, I will embrace the fifteenth Survivor," Ornon intoned formally. "To have even arrived here on this day has proven you among the best, and there will be no shame in leaving the throne to one of you." He stared at Buz while he spoke. "Return now for your weapons. Upon my signal, the conflict will begin!"

Tirri was awaiting Dulok, and he ceremoniously handed the finely honed blade to the prince. He then quitted the courtyard and joined Ayo and Turnivo, who had made a place for him. Lonz smiled at Buz and joined Ornon in his box, for such was his right.

The crowd was hushed, breathless, as they awaited the pleasure of the king. Ornon saw that all was in readiness, and he raised his arm high above his head. He brought it down emphatically, and the multitude screamed as the two warriors approached each other cautiously in the center of the courtyard. For moments they circled like stalking cats, their swords at the ready. Then, quite unexpectedly, Dulok spoke, and the roar of his voice was such that it silenced all in his sphere.

"People of Shadzea, on this most notable of days, hear my words, and heed them!" he shouted. The crowd paused to listen. "Learn of the one you have been proud to call your king these many years, and learn also of one who you would gladly see succeed him!"

Buz could not understand the purpose of this, nor could he care. For a brief moment he spotted an opening, and his skill with the blade was such that he knew he would be able to take advantage of it. True, it was only a small opening, but he needed little more to accomplish his work. With a vicious thrust he drove the tip of his blade toward Dulok's shoulder, and when he pulled it back he saw that he had drawn blood. The throng, temporarily mesmerized by Dulok's words, cheered lustily at their champion's move. The startled Dulok clamped his fingers over the gash and leaped back. It was merely a superficial wound, but he cursed himself for his temporary lack of attention. He swore it would not happen again, even in light of what he must do.

The crowd continued to cheer, and the smiling Buz took a moment to gaze in the direction of Dhela, who smiled and nodded knowingly. He then turned his attention back to Dulok, who he expected to see falling to his knees. He had planned at that instant to administer the death blow, so that none would question why one such as Dulok could have died from a flesh wound. But no cringing, dazed foe awaited Buz. Instead there stood a grim, determined fighter, his wound all but forgotten. He approached Buz slowly, and in his steely eyes the first son could read his own sentence of death. Buz retreated so quickly that one might have thought he was running. He managed a last, pleading glance at Dhela, but the beautiful young woman still smiled, and this time Buz knew that the pleasantry was not for him.

Dhela had haunted the corridors of the palace ever since Buz's return from his Trial of Death. So ambitious was she that she would seek any bit of knowledge to help further her cause, and that of Korb. She had learned of Buz's shadowy night caller, but had only a vague idea of what transpired in his chamber. On the night of Korb's death she finally realized what was afoot, but she could not warn her champion in time. She hated Buz for his misdeeds, and she would have revealed his deceit, but for the first time in her life she had experienced a new emotion: pity. She pitied Dulok for the scorn he was forced to endure, and her greatest desire was to see Buz suffer at the hands of the twentieth son. It was she who had warned Turnivo on the night the demon was sent to Dulok. The phial she had given Buz contained harmless colored water. The confidence that it had given the first son was such that he had refrained from any further attempts on Dulok's life. Now she too would reap the rewards of her vengeance on that day.

"On the night preceding his own final conflict," continued Dulok as he followed the helpless Buz around the courtyard, "Ornon employed ensorcellment to destroy one who would have met him here, and perhaps defeated him. A sorcerer, once an acolyte of Sothor himself, dwelt here then, and until only days ago he has sojourned among you!"

The red priests gasped, for no greater affront to Doj and Bao could be committed. Dulok caught up to Buz and thrust his blade at the coward, who desperately parried the toying strokes. Dulok continued:

"Ornon's accomplishments through his years of rule are duly noted, and many are quite worthy. But in

236

disobedience of past traditions and laws Ornon took a lover, a handmaiden of the queen named Ashmala." The queen gasped, while Buz temporarily went on the offensive and wielded a series of lusty strokes at Dulok, which he skillfully fended off.

"Ashmala," Dulok went on, "was a sick woman, and she became obsessed with the idea of bearing the future Survivor. By devious means she saw to it that she was selected as one of the fifty for the Mating Week, even though her *time* fell prior to this. Ornon came to Ashmala's chamber upon his return from the City of Gods, and despite the strict, irrevocable laws governing this, he planted his seed in her days before the commencement of the Mating Week!"

Ornon rose to his feet, the fires of unquenchable hatred burning in his eyes as he glared at his twentieth son. The crowd gasped at these revelations, and they awaited more, but none were immediately forthcoming. The desperate Buz vigorously renewed his attack, but after a few skillful parries Dulok swung his sword mightily, and Buz's own blade was driven from his hand. He scampered to retrieve it, while Zummek, the council elder, rose and addressed Dulok.

"If this be as you say, and the seed of Ornon was planted in the mother of Buz prior to the Mating Week, then by law he is not one of the Twenty, and as such cannot compete for the right of Survivor!"

"By Shadzean law this is true!" replied Dulok loudly. "But there is more. The seed that became Buz *was* planted early, but not by Ornon! *Buz is not Ornon's son!*"

Silence engulfed the astonished crowd. Buz, who had stooped to one knee to retrieve his weapon, stared disbelievingly at his foe, as well as at Lonz, whose face had whitened appreciably. Ornon, enraged beyond comprehension, leaped from the box and glared venomously at Dulok.

"He lies!" the king screamed. "He is mad!"

"He speaks the truth!" shouted a voice from the benches. It was Ayo. "Return to your tainted throne, and let us hear him!"

The gathering shouted their approval at the red priest's order. Ornon returned to his box and seated himself, while those closest to him moved away in disgust.

"Ayo can relate this portion to you firsthand," shouted Dulok. "Listen!"

"More than twenty-four years ago," began Ayo, "I arrived in the City of Kings many days prior to the Mating Week. With me were other priests, there to lend holy sanction to the proceedings. The woman Ashmala's *time* came and went before Ornon's return. Accordingly, she seduced one of our own number, a priest named Delk, who confided his sin to me. Years later, driven mad by guilt, Delk desecrated the Temple of Doj, and for his action he was exiled to the City of Madness. Buz is the son of Delk!"

Few eyes had been on Buz, few save Dulok's. What slender thread of sanity that had held together his evil mind these many years had been broken with this last revelation, and he could bear no more. He wielded his sword in wild strokes as he bore down on Dulok. He shrieked loudly, and his eyes bulged from their sockets. Dulok sidestepped the headlong rush, and with a mighty swing of his own blade he severed the left foot of the howling madman. Buz crumpled to the ground and stared disbelievingly at the spurting appendage, while some among the witnesses swooned. Dulok continued to address them as though nothing had occurred.

"Buz murdered Vassoe at the bottom of Lake Porsat during the first of the Princes' Trials," he told them. "I witnessed this, but said nothing. How he survived the second trial the gods alone know, but in the City of Madness he was given refuge, and he spent seven days in comfort and luxury. This was arranged by Lonz, his good mentor."

Lonz cringed in his seat, while all gazed at him hatefully. Dulok continued:

"It was in the City of Madness that I learned much of what I know, that which Ayo only confirmed later on. The woman Ashmala came to me, and—"

"But that is impossible!" screamed Ornon as he leaped from his seat. "I had—!" He paused.

"You had her killed, or so you thought!" Dulok completed the sentence. "She despised caring for Buz, and her madness worsened each day. Eventually you assigned a guard to escort her to a distant province, where she was to be murdered, for you feared she would reveal your indiscretions. But this fellow took pity on her, and he deposited her at the gates of the City of Madness. She sought me out during the third Princes' Trial, and in a moment of coherence she told all. She despises you, and was ashamed for what she had done."

The people glared at Ornon, while the crippled Buz crawled upon the floor of the courtyard and gibbered madly.

"To succeed in his Trial of Death," Dulok went on, "Buz made a pact with Blotono, the pirate chieftain. Blotono would abduct Sallia, and Buz would then follow

239

them to the City of Rogues, where he would stage a daring rescue. He swore to you that he would negotiate the Terven Marshes, but instead he employed a galley and departed on a leisurely cruise along the coast, while Sallia suffered. He promised you Blotono's head, but would have brought you the head of another. He only acquired the pirate's head after knifing him in the back. I traveled through the Terven Marshes to assure Sallia's safety, and together we learned of this deceit."

"Why then did you allow Buz to return in triumph?" shouted Ornon. "Surely you must be mad!"

"I thought him mad too," Sallia cried, "and I despised him for it, because my shame was unbearable. Now I understand, as all of you soon will; especially you, *Sire!* Continue, my prince!"

"Ornon sent his sorcerer to Buz, and for years he dabbled in the black arts during the late hours. My return from the Trial of Death constituted a serious threat to their ambitions, so with Buz gone his mentor took it upon himself to try and destroy me. He had the sorcerer send a demon to my quarters, but I had already departed to succor Sallia, and the unfortunate Qual was left to suffer my fate." Lonz attempted to depart the box, but the sharpened blade of a nearby witness kept him in his seat. "All blamed me," Dulok continued, "and certainly the evidence was condemning. But I could not reveal where I had been, so I chose to suffer your scorn. The demon was then released on Korb, and again I was blamed. But some weeks ago the demon came to me, and were it not for Turnivo, son of Ayo, I too would have been killed. With the Stone of Bao he destroyed the thing, and then, with myself accompanying him, we visited the chamber of Buz, where the sorcerer sat in ecstatic mind-lock with the false prince. Turnivo raised the stone, and the sorcerer, *Ornon's sorcerer*, joined his master in Esh!"

The red priests stared in disbelief at Turnivo and Ayo, for to remove the stone from its holy place was a blasphemy. But a curt nod from the head priest assured all that Ayo's deception was justified.

"Death to Ornon! Death to Ornon!" The chant was started by one, but shortly it spread through the populace. His misdeeds had brought despair and death to too many, and for too long.

Zummek rose and silenced the people as best he could. He then addressed Dulok:

"You have known many of these facts for years, yet you chose to remain silent until now. What is the reason?"

"The reason for my actions," Dulok announced, "is perhaps my own greatest indiscretion. I dearly loved the woman who bore me, and felt that our separation was unjust. After years of sadness, I discovered a way by which I was able to visit her and spend some joyous moments. I realize this is conduct unbefitting a prince of Shadzea, and that it is in violation of our traditions; but I could not help it, and of this I plead my guilt. Buz discovered my actions, and he advised Ornon. They followed me to the scullery one night, and before my eyes, the eyes of a child, your brave king drove a sword into the gentle woman's heart, while Buz stood by and laughed with glee. On her still warm body I swore vengeance, and only on this day could my vengeance be consummated!"

"Death to Ornon! Death to Ornon!" The chant began again, and it rose in a deafening crescendo at this final revelation of Ornon's cowardly, inhuman act. The gibbering, bloody maniac that was Buz still gripped his sword, and with a final effort he crawled toward Dulok and attempted to skewer him. The sword, the bloodied hand still clutching it, flew halfway across the courtyard, and the gore that spurted from the mangled wrist spattered on Dulok's body. With his heel he flattened Buz on the stones, and he drove the point of his sword into the jugular. He then pulled the well-honed edge toward him, and Buz's entrails spilled forth from the foot long gash. Dulok cast his sword away, and with a fire in his eyes that reflected the madness of one who had suffered much while awaiting this final day of judgement, he tore the body open and thrust his hand within. He fumbled for a moment, and with a violent yank he pulled free the still warm heart of the despised Buz.

"*Death to Ornon!*" the crowd continued, and the king sat as if paralyzed. The wild-eyed Dulok strode toward the king's box, the dripping organ in his hand. Lonz rose to his feet and attempted to quit the box, but the enraged citizenry would have none of this. Numerous blades pierced his body, and he slumped to his chair, his black soul joined as one with Buz on its journey to Esh.

"*See, Ornon, see!*" Dulok shrieked. "*See, my father! I am the fifteenth Survivor! Come and embrace me! Come, my father, for I bear you something from one named Daynea!*"

"Death to Ornon! Death to Ornon!" the frenzied assembly roared.

The king rose up and walked, trancelike, toward his twentieth son. He held out his arms, and he would have embraced his successor; but the crazed engine of death that was Dulok brushed the arms aside. With a mighty effort he tore open the jaws of the king and thrust the putrid heart of Buz deep into his throat. Ornon gagged and sputtered, and he fought desperately as his proximity to death brought forth reserves of untold strength. But even this, reputedly one of Shadzea's strongest rulers, was no match for the power contained in the vengeance-starved person of Dulok. His flesh turned a ghastly purple, and with a final, convulsive shudder the fourteenth Survivor, the king of Shadzea, was dead.

CHAPTER EIGHTEEN

THE KING OF SHADZEA

Those who cared for him the most poured out into the courtyard to be at Dulok's side. There was Tirri, Ayo and Turnivo, and even Dhela. But most of all there was Sallia, who, despite the gore that covered the prince, hugged his quaking body closely to her. The hatred and anger that had been pent up inside of him for so many years had been released within minutes, in a torrent of fury and horror the like of which none in that courtyard had ever before witnessed, nor would ever again. Slowly she felt the rage leave him, and the overwhelming mental exhaustion brought him to his knees. Tirri and Turnivo assisted in seeing that he was comfortable. Though many were shocked by the deeds he had perpetrated, they nonetheless believed that it was nothing more than the deceitful fiends had deserved.

The pall of silence that had fallen across the gathering was now broken as one by one they realized that Dulok, the fifteenth Survivor, was also the king of Shadzea. They began to shout his name over and over, until the deafening roar could be heard throughout the City of

Kings. All were now aware that the new Survivor was known, but none without the courtyard were cognizant of Ornon's death.

Zummek and the others of the council approached Dulok, for traditionally it was required that the ceremony be closed. The Rite of the Twenty, which had begun so long ago with the Mating Week, was now ended, and only one stood, as was the custom. But there were extenuating factors that puzzled Zummek, and he feared that there would be difficulty in resolving them. He gazed upon the new Survivor, and Dulok, who had since regained his senses, smiled grimly as he observed the questioning look on the elder's face.

"You are in a quandry, Zummek," he offered. "Here before you stands the last remaining prince of Shadzea, the Survivor. Yet his attainment is marred by questionable practices, of which any singular one would have disqualified him at the time. And now, as a final atrocity, he destroys the king, his own father. You know not whether to call for my crown or order my execution."

"There is no doubt that those you slew here this day were deserving of nothing less for their common disregard of decency and the traditions of the ancestors," Zummek began. "And yet—"

"Say no more, Zummek," Dulok interrupted, "for I have no intention of accepting the crown. What I did over the years I did for my own personal reasons, for the vengeance of my mother's brutal death. I wish to leave the City of Kings, perhaps even Shadzea itself. This will solve your problems, will it not?"

"But—but this is unheard of!" Zummek blustered. "Never before has Shadzea been without a Survivor to rule. What shall we do? Who—?"

"Shadzea has a Survivor to rule her!" Dulok announced, and the many witnesses, who had quieted, strained to hear his words. "Ayo returned to the City of Gods after the Birth of Princes with the undesirable infants for Doj and Bao. Knowing what he did regarding Delk, he appropriated the first male child born after myself and took it to his home. His infant son had recently died, leaving his wife with a heavy heart. They raised the child as their own, with only Delk, a dear friend of Ayo, sharing the secret. Ayo made certain that the boy learned of his birthright as soon as he was old enough to understand. He cared little, for he loved his adopted parents, even though he understood what the future might hold. He would only have come forward had Buz attained Survivor, for both he and his father knew that this would be wrong. I learned of him from Ashmala, who had long since encountered Delk in the City of Madness. I give you Turnivo, *the twentieth son of Ornon!*"

All eyes turned to the fine-looking young man who stood at Dulok's side. Even Sallia was shocked by this revelation, for Ayo had not advised her of this. She now understood why Dulok had chosen to share his lifelong secret with them. Zummek stared disbelievingly for long moments, before finding his tongue.

"But this would not be valid!" he protested. "What of the proper training? What of the Princes' Trials?"

"I personally accompanied Turnivo to the site of the first three trials myself," offered Ayo. "There, within days of the others, he satisfied each ritual. As his Trial of Death he journeyed to the Forest of Sothor, and what was accomplished there alongside Dulok is now legend. Turnivo has more than fulfilled his requirements, and is worthy of being proclaimed Survivor!"

"Turnivo!" shouted Dulok, and the assemblage echoed his cry. Within minutes a new name filled the streets of the city, and all wondered at the strange events transpiring within the courtyard. Zummek himself was as bewildered as much of the citizenry, and he consulted hastily with the council so that some decision might be reached.

"The council and I agree that all appears to be within its proper bounds," Zummek finally announced. "We are pleased to accept Turnivo, the twentieth son of Ornon, as the new king of Shadzea!"

The Shadzean guard quickly surrounded their new charge to protect him, or Turnivo and his friends would have been crushed by the onslaught of well-wishers. Those of the city poured forth from the palace to spread the news in the streets, while those from distant provinces returned to their homes to advise their people. Ayo accompanied Turnivo into the palace, while Tirri and Sallia assisted Dulok to his own quarters, and under Sallia's watchful eye the fatigued prince was made to rest. He needed little coaxing.

The palace bustled with activity for the next few days, for Turnivo had purposely delayed the ceremony that would proclaim him king in order to await the recovery of his friend. He spent much of those days sequestered with the Shadzean council, for he thought it best that they understood his plans for reform of the kingdom beforehand. He was correct, for they argued vehemently against any break in the traditions that had stood for more than four hundred years. But in the end the council grumblingly acceded, for they were to learn that the will of this young, determined man was strong.

On the eve of the ceremony, Turnivo visited Dulok in his quarters, and the two talked at length. Sallia had left to spend time with Dhela, whom she had come to hold dear as a sister since the day of the Reckoning. Her experiences had wrought a drastic change in Dhela, and the thought of her past ambitions repulsed her. She had tried to fade quietly from the scene that afternoon, but Turnivo sought her out, for he now knew that it was Dhela who had brought him the warning of Dulok's peril weeks earlier. In the past few days he saw her as often as possible, and any could tell by the look in their eyes that they were slowly becoming enamored of each other.

"I apologize for not having stopped by sooner, my friend," Turnivo began. "Affairs of state already begin to tax me. I wonder now if I should have remained silent regarding my birth."

"And leave this all to me?" Dulok exclaimed in mock horror. "No, Highness; I have not the temperament nor the desire to rule. Did the council blanch at your proposals?"

"Of course, but I left them no choice. The ways of Shadzea are the ways of the past. They argued that the old ways have kept them strong and unconquered for hundreds of years. I asked them over whom did we show our strength? Distant provinces that care little of what occurs here? And who would attempt to conquer Shadzea? It is a barren, inhospitable land for hundreds of miles in all directions, surely of little interest to anyone who might even know of it. Within our boundaries lies the northern forest, a lush, fertile place. Even now the priests travel there to cleanse it of the filth that pervaded it for so long. In the future I will have a city built there, and perhaps we will discover new neighbors beyond it."

"What did you inform them regarding the Rite of the Twenty?" Dulok asked.

"This was the hardest for them to accept. The Rite of the Twenty will be done away with. I will choose a queen when I am ready, and it will be for love. The most worthy offspring will eventually rule. Human sacrifices to Doj and Bao will be no more. My father has convinced the priests that such is not the wish of the gods. Yes, my friend, Shadzea will be different, and I pray it will be for the better."

"I too will pray for you," said Dulok.

"But won't you remain here?" Turnivo pleaded. "I greatly need your guidance, and your support."

Dulok shook his head. "I have spent most of my life within these walls preparing for something that I did not desire, but had to attain. Great tragedy has befallen me in the City of Kings, but I have also found great love. I wish to take Sallia from here, and this, more than anything, is her desire also."

"I understand, Dulok, and I wish you well. Perhaps I even envy you a bit. Know that you are always welcome here. But where will you go?"

"Who knows?" he shrugged. "Once I stood atop a high peak in the Torrean Mountains, and I gazed upon a scene of unmatched beauty below me. It is said that nothing exists beyond the Torrean Mountains, but I find this difficult to believe. Perhaps it is there that we shall find peace."

Sallia and Dhela returned to the chamber, and from the light that glowed in Turnivo's eyes, Dulok felt certain that a new queen for Shadzea would not be long in coming. The two left hand in hand, and Sallia followed shortly thereafter, once assured that Dulok was well.

The next morning, before cheering multitudes, Turnivo was proclaimed the new king of Shadzea. But who was to say what meant more to the young king that day, for within hours he was the honored guest at a second ceremony, that in which Sallia became the bride of Dulok. Ayo presided happily over the ritual joining them together in the eyes of the gods.

The remainder of the day brought less joy, for the two would be leaving their numerous friends. Tirri, though a strong youth, wept bitterly at Dulok's departure, but he swore that he would perform his new duties as Turnivo's page admirably. The farewells of the rest were simple and direct, and once all had been said the two rode forth from the City of Kings. They rode south, and they did not look back.

The pair rode for hours in silence, and not until they stopped to rest were words exchanged.

"You appear pensive, my prince," Sallia stated questioningly.

"I caused you much suffering through the years, Sallia," Dulok replied. "Now, with everything over, I lead you into the wilderness, to where only the gods know. I feel I am being unfair."

"Then you hardly know me, Dulok, for I would follow you anywhere. It too is my wish, my desire. We have been prisoners all our lives, and now we are free! Were we to die in some unknown land, it will at least have been a place that we came to of our own accord. We are free, and we are together. This is all that matters."

"I love you, my flower, and I swear to you that we will find even greater joy somewhere."

They departed, and once more they rode in silence, each lost in deep thought. They did not know if they could even reach the land beyond the Torrean Mountains. If they did, they had no idea what they would find there.

They did not care.

FIVE TITILLATING HORROR FICTION FANTASIES FROM ZEBRA

READ THESE ZEBRA BEST SELLERS

THE BIG NEEDLE   (512, $2.25)
by Ken Follett
Innocent people were being terrorized, homes were being destroyed—and all too often—because the most powerful organization in the world was thirsting for one man's blood. By the author of *The Eye of the Needle*.

NEW YORK ONE   (556, $2.25)
by Lawrence Levine
Buried deep within the tunnels of Grand Central Station lies the most powerful money center of the world. Only a handful of people knows it exists—and one of them wants it destroyed!

ERUPTION   (614, $2.75)
by Paul Patchick
For fifty years the volcano lay dorment, smoldering, bubbling, building. Now there was no stopping it from becoming the most destructive eruption ever to hit the western hemisphere—or anywhere else in the entire world!

DONAHUE!   (570, $2.25)
by Jason Bonderoff
The intimate and revealing biography of Americas #1 daytime TV host—his life, his loves, and the issues and answers behind the Donahue legend.

Available wherever paperbacks are sold, or order direct from the Publisher. Send cover price plus 50¢ per copy for mailing and handling to Zebra Books, 21 East 40th Street, New York, N.Y. 10016. DO NOT SEND CASH!

DISASTER NOVELS